Anonymous

**The Fireworshippers and Dermot McMurrough**

Two Dramas

Anonymous

**The Fireworshippers and Dermot McMurrough**
*Two Dramas*

ISBN/EAN: 9783337256616

Printed in Europe, USA, Canada, Australia, Japan

Cover: Foto ©Andreas Hilbeck / pixelio.de

More available books at **www.hansebooks.com**

# THE

# FIREWORSHIPPERS.

A Drama.

"PROSPECTOR" PRINT.

DEL NORTE,

COLORDAO.

1882.

# THE FIREWORSHIPPERS.

## A Drama.

ZOROTUS.—The High Priest.

PROTILAHAN.—The reigning King.

SABER.—Nephew of the King, afterward King Kuros.

EL KOHATH.—Magician and physician to the King.

ACKBAH.—Chief of guards.

SELSUS.—One of the guard, afterward Chief.

NAROTH.—Lord Chamberlain to the King.

ROFUS.—Commander of the insurgent people.

ALTHEA.—Saber's Cousin, and his betrothed wife.

MAIDA.—Mother of Althea.

HIGH PRIESTESS, of Vestal Temple.

PRIESTESSES, Virgins, Guards, Heralds, Soldiers and Citizens.

# THE FIREWORSHIPPERS.

## 𝔄 𝔇𝔯𝔞𝔪𝔞.

---

## PART FIRST.

### SCENE 1ST.

ZOROTUS.—[*The Priest of Fire, discovered at the Altar of the Great Temple of the Sun performing the rites of worship, the sacred fire burning before him, talking to himself*].

O, thou invisible spirit of life! Dost thou dwell in the flame, or art thou in the winds that bear health and strength throughout the world. The sun riseth, and the darkness, with its attending demons, flee before it. The birds and beasts of the field waken in gladness at his coming, and man riseth refreshed and· hasteneth to his labour. Without thee the earth would be a dark and barren desert. Thou art the source of life, and of all that live or move or creep. O, thou spirit of life, incomprehensible! My soul longs to love and know thee. Now do I the service of the temple, and hence will I take of this fire to warm and feed the people. [*He goes out with firebrand.*]

### SCENE 2ND.

SABER.—[*A young man appointed to do the work of the temple service. In the garden of the temple, talking to himself*].

Alas, what dire and fateful lot is mine. Doomed in youth's prime to be in all things, but the knowledge that I am not, an old and worn-out priest. Alien to the priesthood, I am selected to fill the space of one who died and left no one of priestly blood to fill the place ; and, according to this thrice accursed law, I, being alien, must never enter that blessed and happy state of matrimony. O, the hopeless misery of my condition. O, Althea! light of my soul! I shall never see thee again, or hold thee in my embrace. Is it not better to rush into that unseen world that is beyond this life, if such there be. I will suffer on. Ha! I hear the footsteps of the arch fiend of this most terrible place, the high priest of the sacred fire.

*[Enter Zorotus.]*

ZOROTUS.—My son, thou art favoured high above thy fellows. Glad am I to greet thee, and assist thee in learning more of thy duties. Come, we will away to our duties, and in pleasant converse will review the hidden traditions of our most sacred calling.

SABER.—Father, I must tell thee that I am not pleased to follow this the calling which our mighty King hath set me on. Canst thou not speak, and have this cruel edict changed, and have a youth more proper far than I to minister to this temple. Thou knowest who I am, and what I am. I, the former Monarch's son. That father kind and good, whose every word now cometh back to me, like daggers cutting through my soul. O, let me go, and to the far off land will I go, and vex the King no more. I want not mine own heritage, the kingly crown of Gheba. Protilihan hath it, and I feel, I know, that his brother's blood doth stain his hands. O, priest, have mercy, bid me go, and in some other land, live out the little meed of happiness vouchsafed e'en to the slave.

ZOROTUS.—Boy, thou speakest nonsense, thou rail'st like a fool. Is there a man so high in all this land that doth not bow unto the priest. Thou art a wise and proper youth. Thy uncle knoweth best for thee. He hath thy proper welfare well at heart. Be wise, my son. Take up thy duties here, and be content. There is no higher, nobler part in life than service in this temple. Besides, I have no power to change the purpose of the King. Thou knowest him, and know the stern unchanging will he hath. When he fixeth his mind, then woe to him that seeks to thwart his purpose.

SABER.—I will not, cannot here abide. 'Tis death! Yea, worse, a lingering misery, to which e'en death itself would be a welcome change, I must away. Let me go hence.

ZOROTUS.—Nay, boy, listen. Since you the full truth must know. I am compelled on pain of death to keep you here, or else, if thou wilt not be obedient to my commands, which I fain would make entreaties, then to the lowest dungeon must thou go. Loth am I to tell thee, for I love thee well. But thou must here abide, and, abiding, must appear content.

SABER.—I will not. Cast me into the lowest pit that fiendish malice can devise. Aye! put on me chains, and drag me in the dust, but let me not seem to be content with this most vile and loathsome prison. ·

ZOROTUS.—O, son, think on this before thou speakest thus. This free air, unshackled limbs, the light of day, and wholesome food, and songs of birds, and all that fair and pleasant is, and thou art in the first young blush of youth. Thou thinkest not how fair is all the earth, how sweet the pleasant light of day until thou art deprived of them. I see thou knowest all. How that the King is envious of thy life. How that around these temple walls are hired hordes of men who know no impulse save the King's command, who feel no interest save what he doth feel. 'Tis better to be a priest, and have the comforts of this life, than grope and pine in yonder fateful prison cell. Then, if thou art in there cast, who knoweth but in the dark and murderous midnight hour, his hired minions may do the bloody work they dare not in here do. This ground is sacred. Thou also wilt be sacred from all harm when thou doth take the vow. Shall I now receive thy vow?

SABER.—I will not take the vow. Go, bid the vile usurping murderer do his worst.

ZOROTUS.—Saber, thou art mad. O think of her who plighted thee her maiden vow, how would her heart be crushed to think of thee as racked and torn in yonder prison wall.

SABER.—Away, and mock me not, nor add a keener pang than any torture demons can apply. Think of Althea! Do I not think of her until my veins run hot with fiery blood. O, better far that I should die. Then would a tender memory of him who nobly refused to live a craven dog rather than die a man, come o'er her waking hours, and in her dreams would I then live again. Live, aye live, a brighter memory far, than would the knowledge that a golden crown had pressed this brow, made ignoble by a fear of all that Protilahan could do. O noble life. To live on and on in memories hallowed by a love more strong than king with murderous minions at his back.

ZOROTUS.—O, boy, would I had not lived to see this day. Fain would I, old and worn, and nothing strong to bind me to this world, lay down my life for thee. I must to the presence of the King and tell him all, and first take thee to the prison wall.

[*Both go out*].

### SCENE 3RD.

[*In King Protilahan's audience chamber. The King seated on his throne, attendants and chamberlains kneeling before him.*]

KING.—Depart. Leave me alone.

[*Attendants and chamberlains go out bowing.*]

KING.—[*Speaking to himself.*] Blood, blood, always blood, everywhere. I see it when the lowering western sky doth hold the glowing sun, ere yet he hasteth to go down, and the river rushing to the sea with strong majestic flow, seemeth to boil and seethe with blood, and when the darkness is broken by the coming day, the eastern sky is crimson with the gory hue. I hear it when the winds do whisper low. The rustling leaves when I do go abroad hiss it in my ear. These cringing minions that surround me seem to whisper while they fawn, each to the other, blood, blood, blood.

Yea, and more blood! Though I slay the mother that bare me, though I plunge the dagger in the breast that gave me life, though I kill my first-born, yet will I be a King. Woe be to him that standeth in my way.

[*Enter Lord Chamberlain. Prostrates himself.*]

CHAMBERLAIN.—O, most mighty, dread monarch.

KING.—Speak slave, what hast thou to say ?

CHAMBERLAIN.—Son of the dread spirit of fire, the great priest of the sacred temple would speak to thee.

[*Chamberlain goes out.*]

KING.—Bid him enter.  [*Zorotus comes in.*]

ZOROTUS.—Peace, life, and happiness to the monarch of this great and mighty realm.

KING.—Most holy priest, speak on ; thou hast important matter in thy mind.  Well do I love the speech of the good and venerable Zorotus.  Speak then, I'll do thy slightest wish.  Thy word is law unto the men of Gheba, from him thou now beholdest to the meanest slave in all this realm.

ZOROTUS.—O, potent King, live on and may thy living bless and comfort each where'er he be that oweth thee *allegiance.*  I have a matter in my mind of much import.

That comely youth, thy brother's son [*King Shudders,*] that thy great behest has made to be a priest.  I come to speak on his behalf.  'Tis much against his will he stayed.  He yearneth for the freedom of the air.  I ask thee to bid me let him go, and speed him to some distant land to live in peace and quiet there.  [*King grows furious, shouts.*]

KING.—Here, Guard !  [*Guard, armed, enters.*]

Guard, call thy fellows.  Take this hoary fiend and cast him in the lower dungeon, and with thy staves beat out his treacherous and seditious brain.  Out with him.  Slay him.

[*Guards seize Zorotus and bind him.*]

ZOROTUS.—O King, woe unto thee.  Never again shalt thou enjoy the blessed rest of sleep.  Live on until thy weary life shall leap from thy torn and wasted frame.  Thy brother's blood is on thy hands, and now the priest of the most sacred temple is slain by thee.

KING.—Out with the traitorous wretch.  Do as I bid thee.

[*Guards bind Zorotus and take him out.*]

## SCENE 4TH.

*[In the house of Maida the mother of Althea.]*

ALTHEA.—O, how can I endure the weary dragging hours. 'Tis now so long a time without a word from Saber. I feel a dread, a nameless fear that I cannot express, a shadowing dread of something I dare not put in words. Last night I dreamed that, walking on the plain without the city wall, I saw him, and behind him stood a shape as it were, a man, unseen by Saber, and as I would draw near would Saber beckon me away, then would this dark ill-favoured man stab at him. Then would I essay to scream, and all would vanish into air; I would then awake, then sleep to dream the same again. Then would I dream that Saber would be King and I his bride. O, mother dear, I cannot long abide this agonizing fear, this dread suspense. Would that I could hear the slightest tidings from him; I know his faithful heart, and know that winged dragon's feet were no swifter, than his to bring him to my side were he alive and well. I much do fear that harm to him may come through the evil-minded King. Thou knowest, mother, what was whispered when the good King, even Saber's father died.

MAIDA.—Hush, child. Thou knowest not the fearful import of what thou speakest. Speak not of the King. But rather think that Saber will soon return to cheer thee with his presence. 'Tis e'en some youthful sport, mayhaps the chase. He haply seeketh in his rocky haunt the wild boar of Catharia, or chancing this, some fancy of a slight that unwittingly thou hast given. Well I remember when thy sire and I were as thou and Saber art. How that by times he would affect to leave me and stay away, then return to be far more the ardent charmer of my life. Let not the ardour of thy youthful fancy cast thee into miserable doubt. Saber will return.

ALTHEA.—I fear that it will not be thus. E'en now a dark foreboding fills my mind, as when in full midsummer night, the bright moon is hidden by the thunder clouds and omens of the coming storm do mar the peaceful face of nature. Yet will I be content until I hear. Let us to our duties. *[They go out.]*

## SCENE 5TH.

[*In the King's Council Chamber. The King and Chamberlains, Officers of the household, and Officers. Enter, Lord Chamberlain prostrating himself.*]

CHAMBERLAIN.—O most mighty monarch !

KING.—Speak on slave, and live.

CHAMBERLAIN.—Most mighty potent lord of all the earth. The Chief of Guards would speak with thee.

KING.—Bid the villain enter, and see that all the others retire unto the outer court. [*Chamberlains, &c., retire, and Guard enters.*]

KING.—Ha ! what meanest that foul cudgel that thou bearest, slave ? Speak what meaneth thou.

GUARD [*prostrating himself.*]—Mighty King, I brought it that thou mightest see that I had thy commands borne out. With this did we slay the traitorous priest as thou did'st bid us. See there the impious brain that did'st against thee and thine conspire. And here the blood—

KING.—Villain, stop. One word more of blood, and I will bid the other villains outside tear thee limb from limb. Stop. Thou seem'st a worthy man, and well ▪will I requite thee. See that throughout this mighty realm no one shall hear of how the impious priest did meet his death, and thou Ackbah shalt be the High Priest in his stead, and all the princely revenue of that position shall be thine ; only see that my commands are carried out.

Stay. Thou knowest well the youth Saber. Well, he is to me the choicest thing on earth. Sooner than a hair should fall from his innocent head, would I be as thou madest the vile priest. I put him in the temple, and I fear that harm may come to him. See that he is brought forthwith into my presence. But be sure no harm doth come to him. Understandest thou ?

GUARD.—Yea, O, son of yonder burning sun. Well do I comprehend thee.

KING.—Well, go thou now and bring the lad, or in some well secured refuge place him where no harm will him befall,

Go, Ackbah, and when thou returnest will Ī make thee priest.
[*King goes to his bedchamber, and Ackbah goes out.*]

### SCENE 6TH.

[*Ackbah and three of the guard in the forest.   Time : Night.*]

ACKBAH.—My sturdy men, know ye that this night are our heads as lightly on our bodies, as the leaf, when summer is past, sits on her native bough, ready to fall at the first gust of the coming storm, and, lo, e'en now I hear the roaring thereof. Ye are far more safe than I, for as the lightning's flash spareth the lowly herb, and smiteth the lordly tree, so am I the one to get the first stroke of that tyrant's wrath.

FIRST GUARD.—What art thou above thy fellows that thou, a common soldier, should'st incur the wrath of Protilahan than we.   Thou art puffed up far above thy fellows only in thine own imagination.   My name is Selsus, thine Ackbah, that is the greatest difference that should mark us out. ·

ACKBAH.—Selsus, thou speakest only what thou knowest.
This night before we parted company, did the King inform me that I should fill the place made vacant by· Zorotus.   That I am now second man in all Gheba is true as the potent word of Protilahan can make an edict of the kingdom.   [*Guards mock him by offering sham homage to him.*]

SELSUS.—Well, so have I been appointed higher, but I would not tell thee.   As thou camest out, the cup bearer of the King did constitute me to be the great High Chamberlain. [*Down slaves and do me homage.*]

ACKBAH.—Peace, mock me not.   I would not tell thee, only well I know that this fell secret of the fate of Zorotus must be kept in our four hearts.   But true as word of man, the King did tell me this.   Thou shalt see when to his presence we bear the young man Saber.   Come, friends, let us haste to the temple.   Here I have the keys, and here the King's command unto the guard.   [*They go away.*]

## SCENE 7TH.

[*Before the Great Temple of the Sun.    Selsus and other guards talking.*]

SELSUS.—Friends, I fear me this is dangerous work.  My ancient sire was a man of chosen words of wisdom, and oft hath he told me to seek not the wild boar of Catharia in his den, and here we do the King's behest in a most dangerous and gruesome task.   I would my bones were well out of here and in the remotest province.   I bethink me that what this fellow Ackbah, our comrade hath told us is true, or else the King hath it in mind to make a sport of him until he and we do some most villainous plot.   I would that Ackbah were returned that we might retire and sleep as honest men.

GUARD.—I am not in appetite for this business.   I do much rejoice that none of us save Ackbah knew of the fate of the priest.   You each remember how that Ackbah alone did bear the venerable Zorotus into that inner dungeon, and returning with the bloody club to show the King.   Ah ! but I feel now the stroke of vengeance on my head.  Would I were well out of this most bloody King's employ.

SECOND GUARD.—We are all of the same mind, friend.

SELSUS.—Hist, ah ! the great gate doth open, and by that signal comes Ackbah.

[*Enter Ackbah.*]

ACKBAH.—Men, Away, Linger not, or the wrath of the King is upon ye all.   Flee unto the furthermost mountains and hide ye, for the young man even Saber hath not been found.   He is gone from the temple, and we are as dead men, if we return unto the King without him.   Ah ! that I were already dead, for it is better to face the wild beast deprived of her whelps than to meet the King with such a story.

SELSUS.—Friend Ackbah, cease thy ravings and listen to me.   Thou art but a fool if thou think'st that the King would not be delighted to hear of the death of that young prince.   Thou should'st know that nothing is so much desired by the King as that Saber was as even is Zorotus the priest.   Now Ackbah who can flee from the presence of the King, even, if

thou desirest, where canst thou go, that he will not find thee ?
It is better that thou addest one lie more to the long list thou
hast devised, and tell the King some pretended story. We
are in the waters and we must e'en swim.

ACKBAH.—Selsus, thou art a man of wisdom. Thy words
do calm my reason, and I can see thou art right. Come, my
men, let us away, Selsus speaketh wisdom. If the young man
hath escaped from the temple, many friends will gather to hide
him from the King, and our secret will be safe within our own
hearts. Come. [*Exit Ackbah, Selsus and Guards.*]

### SCENE 8TH.

[*In the King's bedchamber. King, in the robes of the bedchamber, walking.*]

KING.—Oh, Thou sacred spirit of fire. O ! ye gods of Ancient Gheba. Fall upon me and destroy me from the inner
voice that doth haunt me. O, that I were in that burning pit
of pitch that the priest doth tell us of. Now do I believe that
awful tale, that once I did but laugh at, for if such fearful
pangs doth seize on man, steeped as I am to the chin in
brother's blood, aye, and the holy blood of the sacred Priest of
Fire, then what must it be when he goeth to his account. But
I will to bed and sleep. Ha ! now I bethink me. No ! it is
not one of a long list of dreams. The sacred priest did doom
me ne'er to sleep. But it was but the ravings of one in his
dotage. Tired nature e'en must rest, I will to sleep. Spectres
begone ! Fools die, I did not kill the ancient priest. It was
e'en that villain Ackbah. There I will to bed, and to-morrow
will I go to the great temple and make sacrifice, to quell the
wrath of all the angry gods. [*Noise outside.*]

KING.—Ha ; villians what do ye there ? [*Voice outside.*]

VOICE.—O, son of the ancient spirits of Gheba ! mighty
monarch. Thy servant the Lord Chamberlain speaketh. Peace
unto thee. Thy faithful guardsman, even Ackbah would
speak if thou desirest, on urgent business.

KING.—'Tis well, bring my trusted Ackbah in here.

ACKBAH.—[*He enters.*] Most mighty ruler of the land of
Gheba and terror of all the kings of the earth, let not thine

anger rest on thy servant for disturbing thy most peaceful slumber.

KING.—Good Ackbah, well do I hold thee in most high esteem as my trusted friend, Speak, what tidings bearest thou.

ACKBAH.—Most sovereign lord. Thy servant doth dare not look from the dust. Thou biddest me bring the young man even Saber, and so I essayed to do, but never was a youth of so rash a temper, when we got with him to the portal of the temple, with a cutlass did he fall upon us with such a heat that we were fain to flee, not desiring to draw a drop of princely blood, but he bore upon me alone, and would have slain me, so in very peril of my life did I draw my sword, not intending to give him hurt only ward him off, but in the darkness, did he run upon my sword and was slain. O, King do as thou wilt with me, but let the guard escape for they were guiltless.

KING.—Ackbah, fear no harm, thou did'st but as any brave man would do. This is a most sorrowful night. Haste thou away and let me weep. But stay, Achbah, I am the King, but I cannot protect thee against the avenger of blood if thou art known to have slain the prince. It is better then that thou and the guard do put the prince's body away as is the custom of the men of Gheba. Arise, then, take the young man's body, place it on the eastern mount and pile thereon the burial stones, and see that thou speakest not of all these things. Away. [*Ackbah goes.*] So more blood to haunt me, one more pale face to rise and frighten sleep and peace away. O, blessed sleep, Thou priceless treasure that the coffers of the King of Gheba cannot buy. The meanest slave that toils in all this land is more blessed far than I. I would that my cunning musicians would play that I might sleep. [*He calls the chamberlain.*] Ho, there [*voice outside*].

VOICE.—Most excellent king! what wilt thou bid thy servant do?

KING.—I would have my most cunning musicians discourse the music of Arabia in the audience hall, so that I may hear them and sleep. [*After a time, the musicians play softly outside. The musicians continue to play while the King continues to walk. Interval—the musicians cease playing, thinking the King asleep.*]

KING.—They think me asleep, and go away to fall asleep themsleves, and find that sweet oblivion denied to me. O that I was the meanest of that vagabond lot of vagrant men. But 'tis only the rush of dire misfortunes that keepeth me from sleep. 'Tis but natural that it should be thus. Now I remember, how that by times before I could not rest. I am surely guiltless of this rash boy's blood. I gave command to these villains to bear him in safety. But, ah, it is the same. There is Kuros, behind him the venerable priest, and then the boy. And they never turn those deathly eyes from me. O, ye gods of the sacred mountains of fire. They come. Back ye dreadful shapes. Away !

[*Voice outside.*]

VOICE.—Noble King.  Did'st thou call thy servant.

KING.—Yea, most excellent chamberlain, bid my faithful physician come in haste; for I would speak to him.

[Interval.—*Voice outside.*]

VOICE.—Mighty King of Gheba, thy faithful servant El Kohath, the mighty physician and magician of the King's household waiteth outside thy bidding.

KING.—Enter most worthy physician.,  [*Enter magician, prostrating himself.*]

EL KOHATH.—Noble successor of the Kings of Gheba. Thy servant will not arise until thou biddest him.

KING.—Arise, good El Kohath, and bid my foul distemper leave me, I sleep not, though I fain would perish that I might slumber, even the shortest space of time. Viie shapes do haunt me, and I cannet drive them away. 'Tis some unwholesome food that frets me, or perchance some humour of the blood.

EL KOHATH.—Nay most worthy King, 'Tis not thy food, nor yet thy blood. I know full well what doth ail thee. Oft do I meet them and as often do I drive them from the earth. 'Tis bad and hideous spirits, that, being banished from paradise, do roam about and vex the good of this living earth. I will drive them away, as the morning driveth the shadows of the night. Then may the blessed sun of sleep shine on thee.

[*The magician begins his incantations. He draws a large circle, and within lights a fire. Talks to himself.* Interval. *Magician at length draws his incantations to a close. He speaks.*]

Now mighty monarch, seek thy couch and I will stay with thee until thou sleepest.

[*King lies down.*]

---

## PART SECOND.

### SCENE 1ST.

[*In* MAIDA'S *House,* ALTHEA *weeping.* MAIDA *trying to comfort her. Time : Night.*]

MAIDA.—Peace child. Dry thy eyes, thy weeping cannot restore Saber to thee if he is lost. I think me that he hath escaped the wrath of the King, by fleeing to some distant land. Is not the way of the merchants open, as thou goest down to Arabia, and the traffic thereon is great ? 'Tis a welcome business to one so full of energy as he. Or, perchance, he is hidden by some loyal friend of his lamented father. Thou knowest that many such there be in this wide land of Gheba. And there be many whosoever, that let harm come to him would never cease to war until they were helpless on the ground. Be brave my daughter, thou art a King's child, and of the royal blood. I feel assured that Saber is safe. Aye, more, safer far, than the good old priest, Zorotus.

ALTHEA.—Nay, my mother, I am far too confident that at this moment Saber is dead. I cannot close mine eyes to sleep but I see his mangled form ; and at times, I see dark rude men who bare him down with swords and staves. Alas, that before the sweetest cup of life is pressed to the lips, it should be turned to the bitterest dregs. O woe is me. [*She weeps.*]

[*Enter servant, prostrating himself.*]

SERVANT.—Most noble mistress. Outside in the outer court cometh an old man who would speak with thee.

MAIDA.—'Tis some wandering mendicant. Supply his wants and bid him go in peace.

SERVANT.—So I did, but he would not go, desiring as he said, to speak to thee in matters that will not await the morn. He seemeth to be a wandering priest or something of that kind.

MAIDA.—Well stand thou near, and let him come.

[*Enter* EL KOHATH *the Magician, in disguise.*]

EL KOHATH [*prostrating himself.*]—Worthy lady, daughter of a long line of noble Kings, and thou fair lady, peace to both of ye. Lady, I would speak to thee if this servant will retire.

[*Servant goes out.*]

MAIDA,—Speak on good father. Thou art a stranger, but thou seemest by thine eyes an honest man, and honest people need not fear to hold converse together.

EL KOHATH.—[*Throwing off his beard and hair. They know him.*]

MAIDA.—Ah, good El Kohath, more of thy changing forms. What meaneth now this shrewd disguise at this late period of the night. Thou art a good man, and speaketh words of wisdom. Thy tidings will be welcome. Speak on El Kohath.

EL KOHATH.—To night I come, and when thou knowest the import of my message, thou wilt not need excuse for my intrusion. I know then that thou, like me, do'st love the land of Gheba, and do'st love the memory of the good Kings who once did rule this land. Thou lovest the worship of the fire, and dost regard with reverence, the holy priest, Zorotus. Thou knowest likewise, the usurper who now sitteth in the King's seat, and thou knowest what is said of the death of good Kuros. Then thou wilt be prepared for what is to follow. I did but just come from the King's palace, and know what vile deeds hath there been done. I tell thee that the King hath slain the good Zorotus, and hath put a vulgar guardsman in his stead. [*The women scream.*] And further, I heard from behind the curtains, the converse of the King with this vile assassin, and I fear me for the young prince, even Saber.

[ALTHEA *falls in a swoon.*]

MAIDA.—O that I should live to see this day. O, thou vile spirit of ambition. How have I suffered from thee. My daughter lieth as one dead, and she shall surely die.

EL KOHATH.—Good Maida. This news must needs be told, and no one else could tell this same save thy servant. But I will give the maiden a draught from this phial, and she will soon recover.

[*He puts the draught between her lips and she moans. Soon the maiden comes to herself, but will not speak, neither be comforted. After a time the Magician goes away leaving the women alone.*]

### SCENE 2ND.

[*In the King's Chamber. Time, Morning. King alone talking to himself.*]

KING.—Dark despair. Hopeless dark despair. Not a ray of light to shine across my way. Not a beam of heat to warm the cheerless caverns of my mind. O, blessed sleep. How I have tossed this weary night through, with sleep a stranger to my eyes. Would I were the meanest slave that toils in yonder dungeon. The veriest wretch hath some release from pain and toil in sleep. But I have none. I know I feel my fate, to suffer on until the spirit within me doth burn out this carcass in perpetual waking. Horrible thought. But I must keep up my Kingly life. [*He calls servant. Enter servant.*]

KING.—Bid the Lord Chamberlain call Ackbah, chief man of the Guards. [*Servant goes away and, after an interval, Ackbah enters.*]

ACKBAH [*prostrating himself.*]—Long live the King of Gheba.

KING.—Ackbah, this day shalt thou be the Great High Priest of the temple. 'Tis the law of Gheba, that the High Priest shall choose the one who shall be priest after him, and if

2

he should fail in this, then shall the other priests make known their choice unto the King, and the King shall set him so des. ignated, over the temple as the Great High Priest. Then shall the priests take him and consecrate him unto the temple service, after the manner of the ancient laws of this land of Gheba. Now I will cause proclamation to be made that the High Priest is dead, and that Ackbah is the one who shall follow him. Go, prepare thyself, and bid Selsus come to me. [*Ackbah rises and retires. After an interval Selsus enters, prostrating himself.*]

KING.—Good Selsus, well have I noted thee, and thy bravery and fidelity to me shall be rewarded. To-day thou art the head man of the Guard in the room of Ackbah. Do thou be faithful and thou shalt have other reward. Thy word shall now go forth. Go bid my herald sound a trumpet and proclaim that the good Zorotus is dead, and that Ackbah is the high priest in his stead.

SELSUS.—Thy servant heareth the words of the King. [*He goes out.*]

### SCENE 3RD.

[*In the great city of the land of Gheba, people standing around. Enter Herald sounding a trumpet. He proclaimeth.*]

HERALD.—Hear all ye people of the Land of Gheba. May the good King of Protilahan live forever. This day he sendeth greeting and wishes of prosperity to the men of Gheba, and maketh proclamation that the good priest Zorotus, hath died, being full of years, and the King commandeth that all men should mourn for the good Zorotus even for the space of the filling of the moon. And he further maketh proclamation that the good and wise Ackbah shall be the High Priest after him. And whoso contrarieth this proclamation shall surely be cut off and all his house. [*The Herald passes on.*]

FIRST CITIZEN.—What think ye aged father of all this, what wonderful and strange things doth happen, when the good Zorotus dieth, and no one knoweth of the place of his burial. Is it not the custom of the land of Gheba, that the dead shall be laid three days on the side of the holy mountain nearest the sun-rise. So that the sacred light of the sun may shine upon him, and light his way to paradise. Yet who have seen the bearers take the body of the sacred priest, and who knoweth of his burial. Speak aged father, and tell us what thou thinkest of these things.

AGED CITIZEN.—My son, these four score years have I walked upon the earth, and I would caution thee not to speak ill of the she wolf's whelps when thou art in the wolf's den. Who hath power in this land of Gheba, save the King. Be wise,'my son and hold thy peace. The good priest Zorotus, well did I know him, for when boys, have we together played. He was old and the spirit of life had died within him. I feel the same myself. Lo, when I lie down I scarce can rise again, and when I meet my friend who hath clung for years to me, he is a stranger, and I know him not. By this know I that it is not strange that old men should fail and die. And Ackbah, it is said, that he is a proper and a learned man. 'Tis known that he doth stand high in the favour of the King. What then? Let us be content, and go our ways in peace, and ask not of the burial of the good Zorotus.

[*Exit citizens talking together*]. [*Enter another Herald making proclamation.*]

HERALD.—Hear all ye men of Gheba. This day hath our Sovereign the King decreed, and this decree changeth not, that on the morrow will this great High Priest of the Temple of the Sun, be consecrated to the work of the temple, and the King commandeth that the people shall abstain from labour on that day, and at the going down of the sun will the priest make sacrifice for the people. [*Herald goes out*].

### SCENE 4TH.

[*In Maida's House. MAIDA talking to herself.*]

MAIDA.—O, that I could bear this heavy burden for my child. She pineth, and weepeth not, so I well know that her grief is of that degree that cannot be assuaged. My heart is broken, from the awful import of these tidings, but I must bear up, for my daughter's sake. O, weep mine eyes, how are the strong and noble perished. [*Enter ALTHEA sorrowful but calm.*

MAIDA.—My child, thou must not give way unto thy grief. Thy sorrows, like the wounds received in battle, will heal up by time.

ALTHEA.—My much honoured mother. The wounds that I have received, like the mortal wounds received in battle, will never heal, but with longer time get more rancorous and deep.

MAIDA.—My child, thou must take up again the burdens of this life and e'en live on, though life itself be a weight that drags thee to the ground. There is a measure of happiness in overcoming these deep sorrows, as well I know.

ALTHEA.—Thou art right. I shall henceforth live to do the most for good I can. Thou knowest of the Temple of the Virgins, how in that holy place, forever separate from the world, with vows of lasting chastity, these noble virgins tend the holy fire, and comfort and relieve the destitute and sick, and in many deeds of kindness and of mercy, live more noble, holy, and worthy of more praise than princesses in the monarch's hall. Nay, cross me not, most loving mother, I am fixed in this my well digested plan, and e'en to-morrow I go and forever leave this outside murderous world.

MAIDA.—Thy words do cut my heart, like swords in battle wound the shrinking flesh. If thou goest there, then can I never see thee more, for when thou entereth the temple door, and take those sacred vows, then never shalt thou come out hence again. No mother, no friends, no home. O, think my child and thinking stay with me, and we will be a comfort and a stay to each lone widowed heart.

ALTHEA.—Most loving mother. Ere I spake to thee, well had I weighed all this. Much as I love thee, yet I see my duty plain. When thou thinkest of me, it will be as of one whom thou knowest is in the line of all the happiness that may come to her on earth, and in the line of duty which runneth by that of happiness. Thou can'st not change my purpose, I am resolved to go.

### SCENE 5TH.

[*In the Temple of the Vestal Virgins. Twenty virgins surrounding the altar, on which is burning the sacred fire.*]

[*Enter High Priestess of the temple, clad in her robes of office, leading* ALTHEA.]

HIGH PRIESTESS.—Holy virgins what is our highest duty ?

FIRST VIRGIN.—To worship and adore the great creative spirit.

HIGH PRIESTESS.—Where dwelleth that creative spirit ?

SECOND VIRGIN.—He is not bounded by space, his habitation hath no bounds, but his presence is manifested in the sacred fire.

HIGH PRIESTESS.—Whence doth all life and being come ?

THIRD VIRGIN.—It cometh from the great spirit, who giveth all good things, and doeth nothing wrong.

HIGH PRIESTESS.—What is our second highest duty ?

FOURTH VIRGIN.—To keep our hearts and bodies pure.

HIGH PRIESTESS.—How can we best keep our hearts and bodies pure ?

FIFTH VIRGIN.—By leaving behind us the world, and all it contains, take our vow of eternal chastity and ever keep it.

HIGH PRIESTESS.—What is our most important duty ?

SIXTH VIRGIN.—To relieve the needy, sick and distressed in every way we can, without coming in contact with the world. Especially and particularly are we to relieve the distressed of our sex.

HIGH PRIESTESS.—What is our common duty ?

SEVENTH VIRGIN.—To maintain the sacred fire in our temple, and never let it die.

HIGH PRIESTESS—[*To* ALTHEA.]—My sister, thou hearest what hath been said. Is thy resolution still to be one of us ?

ALTHEA.—Yea, it is.

HIGH PRIESTESS.—Let the ceremony now proceed. Thou wilt see while the ceremony progresseth, that thou art dead to all the world, and that thy life is henceforth devoted to the temple work.

[*Virgins clothe* ALTHEA *in burial robe, place her in a coffin, and removing a trap in the floor, lower her into a tomb.*]

HIGH PRIESTESS.—Sisters, we must all pass the portal of death. This portal which our sister passeth now, is as impassable back to the world life, as the portal of natural death is. Our sister leaveth friends and home and all earthly things, and henceforth will live another life of chastity, charity, and self-forgetfulness. Arise sister.

[*The coffin is raised and* ALTHEA *rises, and comes out*].

HIGH PRIESTESS.—Now by the power of the sacred spirit that dwelleth in the fire, wilt thou ever devote thyself to the duties of this temple, live as thou hast been instructed, and ever keep this vow?

ALTHEA.—Yea, I will.

[*Music in an adjoining Court of the Temple.*]

[*High Priestess takes a brand of sacred fire and puts it in* ALTHEA'S *hands. Incantations by High Priestess, over the altar of the sacred fire. She throws incense on the fire. The virgins chanting the vestal hymns.*]

---

## PART THIRD.

### SCENE 1ST.

[*In the forest beyond the city, and adjoining the sacred mountain of Gheba. Time, night.* SABER *alone in the forest. Thunder in the distance. Saber talking with himself.*]

SABER.—Ah, 'tis a fearful night! My heart doth die within me. Not that I am alone, and lost, and know not where to obtain food and shelter from the storm. I fear not the forces of nature. I dread not passing the night exposed to the fury of the tempest. Our mother Nature, though rude, is kindly. [*Thunder louder and nearer.*] Hark! It cometh. Well, I fear not the wrath of winds, or thunders. 'Tis my own kindred and my own blood I fear. Why range I these untamed forests, like the wild and hunted beasts? 'Tis because I am my father's son, and he once the mighty King of Gheba. Yea, he was a noble king—too noble and majestic to see the vileness of his brother Protilahan, whom the good King made the captain of the guard, then president of all the governors, not knowing or thinking of the baseness of the villain that he made a man of, that, like the vile and unclean dog, turned and slew the one who cherished him. Oh, thou great and noble Kuros! I love and reverence thee not as the brave soldier, not as the mighty king, but as the loving and kind father. And hear me, thou great spirits of fire, if such there be: I will yet be avenged of Protilahan. [*More thunder.*] I must haste me, and secure a shelter from the storm. Ah! I think me yonder is the flash of a light. I thought not I could be rejoiced at the prospect of deliverance from the storm, when that was the least of all my troubles. Yea, I now see plainly; it is the hovel of some woodman, and he hath a fire already lighted on the hearth. I will go thence, and haply I will also find food, which I have not tasted these two days.

[*He approaches and enters hovel of a hermit-magician, who is seated on the floor, engaged in incantations before the fire. Hermit does not notice the entrance of* SABER, *but continues his ceremonies.*]

HERMIT.—Kiah, ani, solilah, se, kumiah, O, pruolia, santonah, kantuni maithan.

[*Loud thunder without, which the magician does not notice. Wind and rain shake the hovel and roar without, but the magician keeps on with his worship. After continuing for some time in this way, he concludes his rites, and addresses* SABER *without looking up.*]

HERMIT.—My son, why comest thou here and enterest the shrine of the holy fire without invitation?

SABER.—Good father, wist thou not that the storm rageth without, and even the timid hare will seek the dwelling of man when danger threateneth. Besides, I have wandered since two days in the mazes of this forest, and found neither food nor shelter.

HERMIT.—And why should the King's son be a wayfarer of the forest. Doth not thine uncle, the King, have food and shelter for the only son of the great Kuros.

SABER [*prostrating himself*].—O, holy hermit of the sacred fire, turn me not back to the vengeance of the bloody King, the usurper Protilahan ; well know I he thirsteth for my blood for no reason only that I should be the lawful King of Gheba.  I see thou knowest me.  Have pity on a poor wandering boy, who hath no friends.

HERMIT [*rising and, lifting* SABER].—Noble Prince, be of good cheer ; ten thousand loyal hearts beat for thee throughout this land, and none more true than mine.  Thou art safe from all the fury of the King.  Fear not.  Seat thyself before this faithful servant, this once sacred fire, and soon thy wants shall be supplied, after which thou shalt rest on yonder fragrant boughs, and by morning's light we will hasten to the caverns in the rocks, where I at times abide.  There is safety.  Only be thyself.  Be brave.  Let nothing trouble thee.  Remember son, that dire vengeance stalketh now behind the cruel usurper. As he turneth this avenging demon turneth, and its deadly clutch hath fastened on him, and his days are numbered.  It would be better that he were plunged into the burning crater of the holy mount of fire.  Saber, thou knowest not, but it is true, that thy friends are rousing all over this land of Gheba. E'en now I hear the hammers of the smiths as they fashion the weapons of war to battle in thy behalf.  Thou shalt be a King and not a usurper.  Thou shalt be called Kuors as was the noble King, thy father.  Noble Prince, eat, sleep, and tomorrow we go forth.

### SCENE 2ND.

[*At the gate of the great Temple of the Sun, in the chief city of the land of Gheba.  Guards and Soldiers awaiting the coming of the High Priest.* SELSUS, *chief man of the Guards, addressing them*].

SELSUS.—Soldiers : To-day ye must prepare for war.  It is rumoured that the young Prince hath fled to the remote Provinces of this great land of Gheba, and is stirring up the people for to war against the King.  Ye cannot choose who to follow but the lawful King.

FIRST SOLDIER.—I would that I could follow the lawful King.

SELSUS.—Villain, what meanest thou. But thou art more fool than villain. Knowest thou not that that ambiguous speech of thine would cost thee that empty head if it contained the brain of a fledgling fowl.

FIRST SOLDIER.—I speak without fear, most noble Selsus. The east wind bringeth up from Arabia not more locusts than true and loyal men to battle for the rightful Prince.

SELSUS.—Seize him, guard. Bind him for the lowest dungeon. 'Tis treason to the lawful King that he doth utter.

*(Guards seize and bind him. Enter* ACKBAH *from the Temple service.)*

ACKBAH—What meaneth this commotion, and this uproar here within the precincts of the holy temple. Ha! why is this most faithful soldier bound. Speak SELSUS. Why is this ?

SELSUS.—He did utter treason against our noble lord, the King. He speaketh blasphemously against his lawful sovereign, even Protilahan, and in favour of some villainous plot that would set the young Prince Saber on the throne. Thou knowest that the young Prince is already dead, and there is no lawful monarch save Protilahan.

ACKBAH.—And thinkest thou, noble Selsus, that to bind this man will stop the treason. Nay, truly, but every man whose hands thou bindest will be twenty men, with tongues to proclaim this treason, as thou callest it, to the utmost bounds of Gheba. But let me hear what this fellow hath to say. Come, friend, what said'st thou.

FIRST SOLDIER.—I said I would I could follow the lawful King.

ACKBAH.—Well, so say I. That is no treason to wish to follow the lawful King. What else said'st thou ?

FIRST SOLDIER.—I said that the east wind bringeth up from Arabia not more locusts than true and loyal men to battle for the lawful King and rightful Prince.

ACKBAH.—Good soldier, so may it come to pass. I hope, with thee, that the rightful Prince of Gheba may have a mighty host of loyal men to follow him into battle. Selsus,

thou hast mistaken this sturdy soldier.   He meaneth right, I
assure thee.   Take off his bands and let him go, I see no cause
for binding him.   I will answer for his good carriage henceforth.   Soldier, stay thou here, while I go into the presence of
the King with the guard.

(*The High Priest and Guards go out.*)

FIRST SOLDIER.—Comrades, I spake as truly as I felt, I
meant to say what SELSUS thought I said.   The day cometh
shortly when I must come to battle for Protilahan or for the
rightful Prince, and I shall go with the son of the noble Kur-
sos.

(*All the soldiers speaking.*)   So will we.

FIRST SOLDIER.—And throughout this land of Gheba, there
goeth up with the smoke of sacrifice, from thousands of
true hearts, a prayer for the safety and well-being of the lawful Prince.   The death of the Prince is but a fickle story by
those arch conspirators.   Yet I think me that this High Priest
is with us, and that when occasion calls, he will be a loyal
friend to the young Prince.   Friends, soon ye must choose between the usurper and the son of the good King Kuros.

SECOND SOLDIER.—It will be but small following that the
usurper will get in the army of Gheba.   I know not how the
people of the land will go, not being familiar with them.   But
I have suffered much from this usurper.   Though but a soldier, and in the lowest rank, yet I feel as much as the King,
my kindred are as dear to me as those of Protilahan.   I was
chosen as a soldier and did serve the good King Kuros for
fourteen years, then by all the law of Gheba was I a free man,
and could go to my home, and to the tilling of the soil, but
with my companions were forced to serve another tale, by
this usurping King.   Comrades, the air trembles to-day with
war.   Not with foreign and alien foes, but with our own
countrymen.   Thou sayest that we must choose between the
usurper and the Prince, I tell thee that we cannot choose.   We
must go with the King, or it will be the worse for us.

[*Trumpet sounds, and shortly* SELSUS *approaches, forms the
men, and all march off.*]

## SCENE 3RD.

[*At the cavern in the rocks on the holy mountain of Gheba, Hermit and Saber discovered in the cavern talking.*]

HERMIT.—Noble Prince, now as thou art in a place of safety and comfort, I will leave thee for a season, first discovering to thee the hiding-place of our provender. And here thou wilt find an altar upon which is burning the sacred fire. As thou art of the royal blood, thou hast a privilege of the priesthood, and it is not unseemly for thee to tend the fires, especially as it is likewise a necessity. See thou that this fire goeth not out. I go hence upon a business of the greatest moment, and haply I will not return for many days. See that thou goest not out of this cavern, or thou canst not find thy course herein again.

SABER.—Good father, hear me. Since I were old enough to walk erect, have I known and loved my beauteous cousin Althea. Happly thou hast never seen her, but she is of the fairest. O, if thou goest near the haunts of men, seek her out and tell her that Saber still lives and still loves her. What care I for life or honour if she be lost to me. But I see a shade of sadness cross thy face. Good hermit, speak, knowest thou aught of her ?

HERMIT.—Son. This may be an important matter to thee, boy as thou art. But greater things far are to be done. Thou art the lawful Prince, the first born of the lawful King, and thy place is taken from thee by usurpation and unholy power. The people must be roused in this land from the mountains even into the sea, and from the great rivers of the plain, even unto the land of Kaldea. The usurper must be overthrown, and thou be valiant and of good courage and all will be well, and since I must tell thee, I go forth to arose the people and call them forth to battle against the vile usurper. And when they are met in battle array, then thou shalt go forth and conquer the false Protilahan.

SABER.—Holy hermit, much I fear me that thou ravest as one out of his mind, what cans't thou, a humble hermit, do to rouse the people against the mighty King of Gheba. Thou would'st incur the wrath of the King and perish miserably. Let me rather go away, and remove a great danger from thee.

HERMIT, [*Prostrating himself*].—Most noble Prince. Thus do I acknowledge thee to be my Sovereign. Be wise and remember that I am not what thou see'st, but I am known to the uttermost parts of this great land, and the people know and regard my words. Ask me not, but consent thou to lead thy people to victory. Thy servant knoweth what he speaketh, and he will send emissaries to every part of the land; we will completely overthrow the false King, so that he shall have no more place in this land forever.

SABER.—Well, holy hermit. If I know thee, then will I consent that thou go forth and I will lead the people against Protilahan. Who art thou?

[*Hermit rises, throws off his grey beard and hair.*]

HERMIT.—I knew thee from thy-birth, and I received thy first breath.

SABER, [*starting back in astonishment.*]—Ah! good El Kohath is it thou, thou old and well tried friend of my noble father, and well hast thou kept thyself that thou were't not as Zorotus [*embraces him.*]

EL KOHATH.—And as I have been a friend to thy great sire, so will I be in my humble way to thee; speak and I will go forth and rouse the people.

SABER.—Go, good El Kohath, and may peace and prosperity go with thee, but I am loath to have one drop of loyal blood shed on my behalf.

EL KOHATH.—It is better that there should be some blood spilt, than that the people should groan under the burdens set upon them by the usurper, and we would be less than men to idly sit and see our people enslaved. Think what would thy father say to see his people thus enslaved.

SABER.—Good El Kohath, thy words fire me. I will lead the people, only let me go with thee and rouse them.

EL KOHATH—Now thou speakest like a king. But 'tis better that I go alone at first, when all things are ready then will we seek thee.

SABER.—My faithful friend, my old instructor, can'st not thou tell me where is Althea. Thou has not been long from the city, and thou knowest. Ah! I see again thy countenance is troubled, speak ; tell me what thou knowest.

EL KOHATH.—As much as I know, thy cousin is in good health, is not in danger, is not in peril from the King, and is in a safe place, further than this I cannot tell thee. Be thou brave and cheerful, and all will be well. Now I leave thee, keep thou here until I return, be that soon or late. I must first hasten to the King, as he laboureth with a bad distemper, Be of good cheer. I depart.

[*El Kohath puts on his disguise and goes.*]

SABER, [*solus.*]—These things do stir my kingly blood within my veins. Well do I trust the good El Kohath, for he was my father's trusted friend. He hath been a most mysterious man, but still he is an honest faithful one, and he is prudent and will keep out of harm. But Oh Althea! where art thou to day? Proudly would I sit upon the throne of Gheba, if thou did'st sit beside me. When the good physician returneth he must tell me what he knoweth of her. I do not like his troubled face, when I first spake of her, I fear me something is not right with her, although he said she was in safety. Well I must content myself and wait until he returneth.

[*Scene closes*].

### SCENE 4TH

[*In the King's palace again—King much enfeebled, and with a wild uncertain air, talks to himself—time, night*].

KING.—O, vile wretch that I am. These four nights hath slumber fled mine eyes. O, that the vile horde of Kings were in the pit of burning pitch, and I with them, 'twould be the lesser torment to be there than cursed with these bloody shapes that haunt me. Back, thou ghastly apparition. Ho, there Chamberlain. [*Voice outside.*]

VOICE.—Mighty King, what desirest thou.

KING.—Bid my good physician El Kohath, come within at once.

VOICE.—Mighty monarch, it shall be done as thou sayest.

[*Interval. Knocking at the portal.*]

KING.—Enter in the name of peace. [*Enter El Kohath.*]

KING.—Good physician, arise. Now must I tell thee that I cannot [slumber, and thy arts and physic do me no benefit; cans't thou not prepare a draught that will cause me to sleep? I die for want of it, yet cannot I close my eyes.

EL KOHATH.—Great monarch, it is not always possible to regulate the humours of a man. The cause still remaineth in him, even if we give the most approved medicines. Get thy mind at ease, and I will stay by thee till morn. Take this potion, and I think that thou wilt sleep. [*He prepares a draught and gives it to the King.*] Here most noble King, take this and I think it will make thee sleep.

[*King takes the draught, which stupefies him, but he does not sleep. EL KOHATH goes out. Scene changes to outside King's bed chamber. EL KOHATH and LORD CHAMBERLAIN engaged in conversing in low, guarded tones.*]

LORD CHAMBERLAIN.—Good physician, how goeth the cause to-day. Whence comest thou?

EL KOHATH [*In great surprise.*].—I come from the presence of the Prince.

LORD CHAMBERLAIN.—Ha! How speakest thou? Man, art thou mad? From the presence of the Prince?

EL KOHATH.—Yea, truly spake I. He is not only in good health, but in safety, and where he can come forth at a moment's warning. All that I fear, is this most serious and unfortunate whim of the girl his cousin.

[*Here EL KOHATH tells how he found Saber, and what followed.*]

LORD CHAMBERLAIN.—Noble physician, had'st thou done me the greatest favour known, thou could'st not have pleased me better. Now is the pathway clear. One brave moment, and the rightful Prince will be seated on the throne. El Kohath, this night must not give place to day before the good cause shall be begun. Let the secret emissaries go forth to the remotest bounds of the kingdom. But what think ye of the humour of the King.

EL KOHATH.—He fareth badly. His misdeeds do lash him to madness. He hath the will to be a villain with a coward's conscience. He will surely go into madness, unless he hath relief. But we must be wise and discreet, or his very madness will miscarry our plan. How standest the army, thinkest thou ?

LORD CHAMBERLAIN.—I have had little occasion to learn. This fellow, Selsus, I am wary of, I fear he is a partizan of the King. So being discreet, I have made no inquiry. I am likewise suspicious of the High Priest Ackbah, although he seemed a far better man than I hoped he was.

EL KOHATH.—I would that I were away, I must needs go myself to-night by way of the plain unto the city of Isan, for the people must be roused, and no one knoweth the men to trust, as I do.

[*Knock at the portal.*] [*Voice.*]

ACKBAH [*outside*].—Noble Chamberlain, I would speak with thee.

LORD CHAMBERLAIN.—Enter, Sacred Priest.

[*Enter Ackbah.*]

ACKBAH.—Peace to thee, noble Chamberlain, and thou most learned Physician.

EL KOHATH.—Peace, Sacred Priest. Speak thy mind fully, we can trust the noble Lord Chamberlain.

ACKBAH.—Well it pleaseth me to find that thou art to be trusted. The good Physician and myself do understand each other fully.

EL KOHATH.—Now, noble Priest tell the Chamberlain thy secret. It is necessary that he should know.

[*Ackbah whispers in the ear of the Lord Chamberlain who is so much overcome with astonishment that he can not speak. After an interval. El Kohath biddeth them farewell and goeth away.*]

LORD CHAMBERLAIN.—Noble Ackbah this most marvellous thing doth take away my mind, yet am I much rejoiced, but one thing remaineth to mar a glorious victory.

ACKBAH.—What is that, worthy friend ?

LORD CHAMBERLAIN.—I mean the whim of the maiden to join herself unto the vestal virgins. Thou knowest the law of Gheba. She cannot come hence again, by reason of her vow, even the King cannot set it aside, neither the High Priest, nor the great assembly of the people, nor the maid herself, nor any eaithly power. This is much more serious than thou thinkest. I know how much the prince is enamoured of the maiden and it must not be that he heareth of this, or he will be as a madman, and cannot lead the people.

ACKBAH.—Hast thou spoken unto El Kohath. He is a man of wonderful wisdom and sagacity.

LORD CHAMBERLAIN.—Yea ! and a most mysterious man. He is a riddle most difficult of solution. I know not his ways, although we have served the King most intimately for many years. Well, upon occasion we will lay this matter before him, and now each must bear his part in the coming struggle. I must watch beside the King until the morning.

ACKBAH.— Dost thou think that he misgives us, or doth he think of any plot ?

LORD CHAMBERLAIN.—Protilahan is a shrewd and cunning man. I am assured that some warning hath been given him. It would be no surprise, for the very winds are laden with the thought of deliverance from the curse of his presence. I fear me that Selsus hath warned him. Yet will we be discreet, and await the coming of the Prince.

ACKBAH.—Doth the King now sleep ? I hear him not, as usually he keepeth the palace full of his roarings.

LORD CHAMBERLAIN.—The Physician hath given him a potion that doth keep him quiet, albeit he sleepeth not. Our cause is not to be won by base murder, or he would never awake or sleep again. It must be too that vengeance smite him here, and the baseness of his own villainy meet him face to face.

ACKBAH.—I must away, and may peace remain with thee.

[*He goes away and the Chamberlain goes in the King's bedchamber.*]

## SCENE 5TH.

*[In the market-place of the city of Isan, in the land of Gheba. Many friends standing about. Enter El Kohath, dressed as a hermit. He addresses the people.]*

HERMIT.— Hear ye men of Isan. Remember ye not the ancient glory of the men of Gheba. How that they went forth to battle, and no people could stand before them, for they were a people who loved their rulers, and they were governed in kindness and moderation. But now, where is the good King Kuros, and who is it that followeth him and sitteth upon his throne? Is it the wise and good son of the King Kuros, who by the ancient law of this land should sit upon the throne? Who setteth burdens upon the people and taketh them to fill his own coffers? Who grindeth the children of Gheba, and setteth taxes on them? It is the usurper. Rise! Rise ye men of Gheba and utterly cast out the vile usurper, for the young Prince still liveth, and waiteth to lead his people against the false King!

*[Great commotion among the people, some shouting and others conversing earnestly together. Hermit is lost in view in the crowd and goes away. Trumpet sounds, and the people begin to array themselves to fight for the young Prince.]*

## PART FOURTH.

### SCENE 1ST.

*[In the camp of the insurgent people of Gheba, in the tent of* ROFUS, *the commander of the people. Other captains and chief men of the army present in uniform. Noise of trumpets without. Enter* EL KOHATH.]*

EL KOHATH.—Mighty chief captains of the land of Gheba, to-day goeth the great work forward. Ye have well done your duty, and a vast army of the people are assembled, impatient to march on to conquer the usurper. But one important step remains to be taken. It is meet that the young prince, the lawful king, should now stand before his people. He is near, and I will now go with the Lord Chamberlain of the King's palace and bring him hither.

3

[EL KOHATH *and* LORD CHAMBERLAIN *go out, and shortly return with* SABER, *clad in the war vestments of the Kings of Gheba. All present do him obeisance. Trumpets sound.*]

EL KOHATH.—Behold your king.

SABER (*as Kuros, the new King*).—Arise, faithful captains. It is my wish that no harm be done to any, save unto the false King. The innocent blood that he has shed be upon his shoulders. Now, good Rofus, what is thy pleasure?

ROFUS.—Valiant leader, let us go forth and permit the people to see thee.

[*They go. Sounds of martial music and shouts outside.*]

EL KOHATH.—Well doth the young prince bear himself. There is inspiration in his presence. When the people go forth under his command, the men who cling to the usurper cannot stand before them. Warder, hath the tent of the young king been prepared?

THE WARDER.—Yea, good physician, all things are in readiness, even to the smaller matters. Likewise hath the King's guard been set.

EL KOHATH.—Thou hast done well. See thou that nothing lacketh, for the Lord Chamberlain and I must return to the King's palace in haste. I am impatient of this day of retribution. The spirits of our ancestors look down to-day with pride upon their children breaking off this galling yoke. Worthy captains, be strong, be valiant, and all will be well.

[*He goes out with Lord Chamberlain. Interval, when the young King and Rofus enter.*]

KUROS.—Captains, ye are the men who were once the well-tried friends of my noble father. Right glad am I to have ye thus around me. Go forth each man unto his place, and cheer the people. Let nothing be done unseemly, but everything as becometh the dignity of the King and the nobles of the land of our fathers. To-day shall be to all coming time a notable day in our history. Good Rofus, hath the guard been set around the encampment?

ROFUS.—Yea, my lord the King.

KUROS.—Hath any tidings been received of the false King, what he doeth?

ROFUS.—There hath but just come in an emissary from the High Priest, Ackbah.

KUROS.—Let him be called.

[*They bring in the spy, who prostrates himself.*]

KUROS.—Speak, friend, what tidings hast thou brought with thee.

SPY.—I thought me there was some dire commotion in the palace of the King, so I sought out the High Priest. He saith that the King hath shown himself to be a resolute man, and one of good courage, that he hath sent forth and gathered together a good army, and that, albeit, he hath serious humours, he goeth forth at the filling of the moon to lead the men of Gheba which he hath called together, and while we yet spake together, lo there came the King's guard and bound Ackbah, and took him to the dungeon. I fear me that it fareth ill with him.

KUROS.—Thou art a faithful man. Guard take this man and let him be clothed and fed, and let him be supplied with what he lacketh.

[*Guard takes the spy out.*]

KUROS—Ye hear what this man saith. Is he an honest man ?

A CAPTAIN.—Yea, my lord, I know him to be a good man.

KUROS.—Then it is a sad thing that Protilahan hath fallen upon good Ackbah. I fear me that he will be slain, as Protilahan hath no scruples to slay any one when the whim doth prompt him.

ROFUS.—Fear not, my lord. The false King is surrounded by spies and enemies, that he hath made from honest men. Let him be accursed for thus turning loyalty and honour into craft and perfidy. But I have great hope of El Kohath, the physician. The King feareth him, and no one else, and the physician will rescue Ackbah.

KUROS.—This tidings doth warn us to be prepared for battle. Protilahan hath the great influence of the army and of all the mighty men. He hath arms and equipments. Let our smiths and armourers be commanded to be diligent. Let all things needful be done.

ROFUS.—It shall be done as thou commandest, noble Prince, and now seek thou thy tent, for thou art wearied with thy journey.

[*All salute the Prince and he retires with Rofus.*]

FIRST CAPTAIN.—Well doth he bear himself. Thou couldst tell that he is more than common born. And methinks that he strongly resembleth the old King, his father.

SECOND CAPTAIN.—Yea, thou speakest right, but it will require much more than pleasant looks to defeat the false King. I know him well, for I was one of the last that held out against him, before I fled into other lands. Protilahan is a great general, and a most courageous man, albeit he is a cowardly villain in murder. I see before us a most deadly struggle, and before the young man sitteth on his father's throne there must be much blood spilt. But I am with the youth, and my life will I gladly lay down to make him King.

THIRD CAPTAIN.—We have all been driven from our homes, and have been outcasts, since this usurper sat upon the throne. Our lives are upon the issue of this combat, for if the usurper should prevail, then would we all miserably die. Death would be sweet if by dying we could deliver our country. Let us be brave and battle for the lawful king.

[*Scene closes*].

## SCENE 2ND.

[*In the lower dungeon of the King's prison, Ackbah in chains, a rush light burning.*]

ACKBAH [*talking to himself. Time, night*].—Chains weigh me down. Walls, shut me in. Cruel murder, crush out my life, but O, thou unchained spirit of liberty, go forth to conquer. Thy home is in the free light and air. Despotism cannot bend thee, nor perfidy enslave thee. Right glad am I to lay down my life that the people may cast off the yoke of the usurper. I cannot hope to escape the vengeance of the King. Yet will the good work go on. It cannot stay, for lo the people are in the field with the true Prince at their head. Fain would I live to see him crowned ; but some must die, and thus prepare the way for the great work.

[*Noise at the door. Door unlocked, and a strange man enters with a drawn sword, and keys of prison in his hand.*]

ACKBAH.—Friend, who art thou? I know thee not.

MAN.—Ha, villain, what matters it that thou knowest me not. I know thee a vile traitor, who warming by the fire of the King, depending on his good favour for all thou hast there, in the security of offices and positions from his hand, doth conspire against his life and kingdom. Approach soldiers. [*Four soldiers come out of the passage.*] Seest thou these trusty soldiers, now what excuse hast thou for thy treason.

ACKBAH.—There is no treason in betraying an usurper and a murderer. Do thy worst. I am prepared.

MAN.—Here soldiers, villains, why hold ye back. Do your duty.

FIRST SOLDIER.—I cannot shed the blood of the Anointed Priest. I will not.

[*All the soldiers speaking*] Nor I. Nor I. Nor I.

MAN.—Comrades retire beyond the area, and come when I call.

[*Soldiers go out. Man shuts the door.*]

MAN.—[*Throwing off beard and armour and displaying* EL KOHATH].

ACKBAH.—O, El Kohath, my friend and deliverer.

EL KOHATH.—Hist. Not a word. These villains cannot be out of hearing of thee. Here let me spill this red liquid on the floor, and on this sword. So. Now let me wrap thee in thy robe. Thus. Now everything for our true King and our land. Good Ackbah, be of good cheer.

[*El Kohath calls soldiers, they return.*]

EL KOHATH [*again in disguise*].—Here, men. Take this body away and do it honour. It is the body of the Priest, though a traitor when living. Bear him to the holy mountain to the eastward, as is the custom with the men of Gheba. I will close the dungeon, and keep the watch until ye return.

[*Soldiers carry off the body of Ackbah.*]

EL KOHATH.—Thus another faithful and true man is delivered from the treachery of the King. Now must I away and assist good Ackbah unto the Temple of the Sun. There he will be safe. Then must another strong and dangerous

move be made.   Then victory.   Then deliverance to the fair
land of Gheba.   Then rightful Prince take the throne.
[*He goes out, locking the door.*]

SCENE 3RD.

[*In the King's private apartment.   King alone, a wild, haggard
look on his face.   Talks to himself*].

KING.—O, treason, perfidy, base, base ingratitude.   My
trusted men, those I have digged from the mire, and placed
high above good men, now turn and seek my life.   Seek my
life ?   It were a noble work to slay me, and remove the cank-
ering conscience  that teareth my vitals, and doth not kill me.
Ackbah, base wretch.   This Numidian that I sent to slay
him, looketh the villian sufficient to do the deed, and he cometh by recommendation of good El Kohath, the only man save
Selsus I dare trust.   So I hope 'tis well done ere this.   But to-
morrow I must lead my army, and I must speak to Selsus,
then consult the physician, and perchance be blessed with
sleep.   Perchance what the old priest said was only the drivel
of his dotage.   I must sleep.   'Tis against the nature of a man
that he sleep not.   Yet, horrible thought, I have not slept
ince Zorotus did curse me.   Ho, there !  [*He calls*].
VOICE [*outside*].—Mighty King of Gheba, thy servant heareth.   What desirest thou ?
KING.—Call Selsus, the chief General of the troops.
VOICE.—Most Noble Lord, I go.

[*Interval—Selsus enters*].

SELSUS [*prostrating himself*].—Mighty King, thy faithful
servant doeth thy bidding.
KING.—Yea, Selsus, I believe thee to be my most trusted
servant.   My confidence in thee is firm and unshaken.   If I
had but the shadow of a doubt, thou would'st not behold to-
morrow's sun.   But I should not speak thus unto one so true.
Selsus, forgive me.   Thy loyalty is true as thy word, which is
truth itself.   I speak but as an old worn and wasted man.
Now, how goeth the preparations for battle ; are m ypeople in
array ?   Are their wants supplied ?
SELSUS.—My lord the King ! all things are well prepared
unto battle.   Thou hast chariots and horsemen, and soldiers

as the leaves of the trees for multitude. The army of the young Prince will flee before them as locusts of the desert.

KING [*startled and terrified*].—Young Prince ? What young Prince ? What sayest thou ?

SELSUS.—The young Prince Saber leadeth the rebellious people.

KING [*gasping*].—Quick, fetch me my good physician ; I die. Stay, good Selsus. 'Tis but the passing of a weakness that often teareth me sore. Go on ; art thou sure of what thou sayest ?

SELSUS.—Mayhaps thy rest hath better not be further broken. I will leave thee and speak with thee after thou resteth.

KING.—Nay ! I command thee to proceed, or forfeit my good confidence. Speak on. What of the young Prince ?

SELSUS.—Well, my trusty spy was in their camp, and saw the young Prince when old Rofus, thy brother's chief General, did present him to the people. And there was great noise of shouting and enthusiasm among them. And he farther saith that a great multitude are with the people, and they have much arms and munitions of war.

KING.—Good Selsus. I know full well old Rofus. He is a great General, and a man most difficult to conquer. We must prepare for a most desperate war. This old General fighteth lustily. I have seen ten men set upon him in battle and he slew them. A most valiant and noble general, I thought him long since dead. Selsus, do thy best, I am but an old man, and if we conquer these rebellious men, then will I leave the kingdom to thee after me, as I have no son to take the inheritance. Good Selsus, I distrust thee not but thou art a youth, and Rofus is old in war. I will lead the people myself. Go forth, prepare my chariot, and meanwhile send my good physician, even El Kohath, for I shall be like one dead unless I slumber.

[*Selsus goes out*].

SCENE 4TH.

[*Same as before, King reclining on his couch.* EL KOHATH *prostrating himself.*]

KING.—Good El Kohath, arise. These are troubled and vicious times. As thou see'st, I am worn and wearied by the vile treasons of my most trusted men. As thou knowest, my people rebel against me, and I must go forth to conquer them or be slain in my palace. I must be refreshed by sleep, or I die, and my people perish at the hands of turbulent and treasonable men who have long been exiled from this land, but now return to stir up strife. First tell me, good physician, if thou knowest, doth this young man Saber join with the rebellious host?

EL KOHATH.—I have been so informed. In fact, I am sure that he leadeth them. But content thy mind, thou need not let thy mind dwell on these things be quiet, and may hap thy slumber will return to thee.

KING.—Go bid the hurricane, Be quiet. Speak to the ravenous beast of the forest, when he rageth with hunger, and soothe him to quietness, then ask me to be quiet. Nay, physician, thou must use the deepest arts, thy greatest skill. I must slumber this night, for to-morrow I lead my people to-battle.

EL KOHATH.—I have but one course left, I needs must use the extreme extent of my ability in magic. 'Tis no common things that rob thee of thy natural slumber. 'Tis the bad spirits, and they must be driven hence. Now I proceed.

[*He builds an altar, bringing materials from the outside. He then puts on his magician's robe, lights the sacred fire, and begins his incantations, the fire burns blue. Noises of strange music out of the altar. Strange sounds from different parts of the apartment. Magician speaks.*]

EL KOHATH.—O King, thou art a wise and great King. Thou knowest not the mystery of mysteries, thou knowest not that slumber leaveth thee for thy bloody deeds. O, King, live forever. O, spirit if thou art bad, leave. O, spirit if good, come forth when I call thee. Live forever, O King.

[*He stops chanting, takes a wand and strikes the altar. A great smoke arises. The Magician speaks.*]

EL KOHATH.—Kai, themo, sai, maithan.

[*Loud thunder. Zorotus the old priest appears in the smoke, and steps toward the King. King seeing him, with a look of great terror throws up his arms and falls back on his couch dead. Instantly all is darkness.*]

## SCENE 5TH.

[*In the great Temple of the Sun.* ACKBAH *and* ZOROTUS *in the priest's chamber talking. Time, about daybreak.*]

ACKBAH.—Holy Priest, this word thou tellest me doth fill me with astonishment. 'Tis true the King did think thee dead, e'en since I showed to him the bloody club ; but I thought not thy appearance would cause him to die.

ZOROTUS.—'Twas his wicked conscience that did accuse him of my murder. He was guilty, and the thought did crowd him to his death. But I must minister to the holy fire. [*He goes out and* EL KOHATH *enters.*]

EL KOHATH.—Good Ackbah, peace be with thee. I have sent trusty men in all haste unto Kuros and unto Rofus. We must prevent the meeting of the King's army with that of the Prince. I have sent unto Kuros to make haste and come hither, and be anointed by the High Priest, as is the custom of the men of Gheba, when a new king is anointed. There is now no cause of war, as the young Prince is the rightful heir, even if the dead King were the lawful monarch. In the meanwhile, do thou send emissaries unto Selsus that the army of the King return unto their homes. I have sent for Naroth, the Lord Chamberlain of the King's house.

[*Interval. Enter* NAROTH.]

NAROTH.—Good Ackbah, my soul is rejoiced to see thee. I thought thee dead.

[*He embraces* ACKBAH.]

ACKBAH.—So I should have been, if it had not been for the sagacity of the great physician El Kohath.

EL KOHATH.—Peace, I did but little. In truth, the soldiers had little mind to do thee hurt. But, friends, I must now away. Make all things ready for the coronation.

[*He goes.*]

NAROTH.—What a most wonderful man is the physician. He is as the changeful sky in the season of the year when the winter departeth ; but he is always good, and nobly true. But tell me, Ackbah, how did the venerable High Priest escape the notice of the King, that he thought him dead ? 'Tis wonderful,—'tis more than wonderful !

ACKBAH.—The story is soon told.  At first, the King Protilahan was very jealous of the young Prince, and secretly
sought to cause his death or drive him to some distant land.
But there were many friends of the old King remaining, and
they cared for the Prince.   They saw in him the true successor
to the throne of Gheba, and mayhap the deliverer of the land
from the oppressions of the King.   Many of the great men who
were near the King, as thou knowest, were the secret friends
of Saber, and while they did homage to Protilahan, did succour
the young man.   Now did the King conceive the plan to put
the youth into the succession of the priesthood, and thus get
rid of him forever.   But thou knowest that the youth, being
enamoured of his cousin, could not brook the life of the priesthood, and thus was Zorotus made to feel the anger of the King.
He commanded me to slay Zorotus, and I dare not disobey the
King.   So we made the plot to take Zorotus to the dungeon,
seem to slay him, then return with plausible stories unto the
King.   This I did, getting a club in the shambles and showing
it to him.   Then I secretly took the High Priest back into the
temple, where he ministered unto the sacred fire, whilst I seemed
to be the High Priest.   No one knew the secret, save myself,
the magician and Zorotus, until it was told to thee that Zorotus
still lived.   Yea, and long may he live, for he is a good and an
holy man.   El Kohath goeth to bring the young King, that he
may be crowned with the ancient golden crown of Gheba, that
containeth the diamond brought from Paradise ; that resteth
in the Temple of the Sun, save when placed upon the head of
the new King by the High Priest, and no man dare so much
as lay hands upon it, save the High Priest.

NAROTH.—Right well hath this been done, for the blood of
the Holy Priest, had it been shed in vain, would have rested
on our people unto the latest generations.   But, shall the dead
usurper be buried in the tomb of the ancient Kings of Gheba ?

ACKBAH.—Yea ; what harm can there be in that.   Protilihan is now dead, and there remaineth not one soul to keep his
name on earth.   He is laid on the holy mountain for three
days, as is the custom with the men of Gheba, and no one
mourneth for him save Selsus, who among all the great men of
the King's house, is faithful unto him.   Had'st thou heard
that the army of Gheba had sworn allegiance unto Kuros,

when they heard of the old King's death? All save Selsus and a few others, have gone unto him. Good Naroth, let us go and offer our worship unto the fire, then go forth.

[*Scene closes.*]

## PART FIFTH.

### SCENE 1ST.

[*In the great Temple of the Sun, in the chief city of Gheba, chief captains, priests, chamberlains and others. The great throne of Gheba with canopy of fine linen over it. Enter a Herald sounding a trumpet.*]

HERALD.—Hear, O ye Chief Captains! Hear, O ye High Priests! Hear, O ye mighty men of Gheba! Now cometh the son of the ancient Kings of Gheba, to sit upon the throne of his fathers. Lo, he cometh, and the earth rejoiceth, and the children of men are made glad by reason thereof. Let him be forever accursed that is not loyal to the great King Kuros, the father of his people, the son of heaven, and the joy of all the earth.

[*Mighty sound of trumpets outside. Enter Zorotus clad in the sacred vestments of the High Priest, and after him the young King clad in sackcloth and followed by Officers and the Lord Chamberlain. Officers behind, bearing the Kingly robes. Music and shouting of the people. Zorotus lights the sacred fire on an altar before the throne. He then ascends unto the throne and commands silence*].

ZOROTUS.—Ye men of Gheba, hearken now unto the words of the High Priest of the sacred temple of fire. To-day there is no King in the land of Gheba. The good King, even the old King Kuros hath died, and hath he left a successor?

NAROTH [*the Lord Chamberlain*].—Yea, most Holy Priest. He hath left a son who is here to-day.

ZOROTUS—Can any man testify unto the young man being the son of the good Kuros.

EL KOHATH.—Yea, most holy priest, I was the physician of the King's house, and I witnessed the birth of the young man, even Saber, who was conceived of the wife of the King Kuros, and I received his first breath.

ZOROTUS.—Knoweth any man aught to the contrary, why this young King should not now be crowned in the presence of this people ?

ROFUS [*Chief General*].—Nay, most Holy Priest. No man hath any reason to object thereto.

ZOROTUS.—Then let the young man be brought hither.

[*They bring Kuros to the foot of the throne.*]

ZOROTOS.—This youth hath not proper raiment for the King of the great land of Gheba.

LORD CHAMBERLAIN.—That showeth that he leaveth all behind him of his past life, and that he cometh into new life, even the life of the King of Gheba. The land of Gheba hath a new robe to put upon him, even the royal vestments of the ancient Kings.

ZOROTUS.—Bring me the royal robes of the Kings of Gheba.

[*They bring the robes and Zorotus puts them upon Kuros, saying :*]

ZOROTUS.—Thus do I clothe thee with the power and authority of the Kings of Gheba.

[*He then removes the canopy from the throne, disclosing the royal crown containing the sacred diamond. He takes the crown in his right hand and with his left takes a brand from the sacred fire, saying :*]

ZOROTUS.—What signification hath this fire ?

A PRIEST.—It is emblematical of the great creator and sustainer of the earth, and of all the men thereon.

[ZOROTUS, *placing the crown on the head of the Prince and seating him on the throne, places the fire brand in his hand and takes a horn of sacred oil from an officer and pours it on his head.*]

ZOROTUS.—In the name of the sacred spirit of fire. In the name of the great land of Gheba. By the word of the High Priest of the Sacred Temple, I now proclaim thee Kuros, the King of Gheba. May thy days be lengthened, and may thy people ever love and serve thee. Long live the King Kuros.

[*Great noise of trumpets and of shouting of the people, all the great men prostrating themselves before him. A herald blows a trumpet and there is silence.. Zorotus feeds the sacred fire and then stands beside the throne. Kuros addresses the people.*]

KUROS.—My people, this day is my heart troubled, for I see a great care for so young a man, to govern this people aright. If I go wrong, it will be made right as soon as I know thereof. I see men here from all parts of my kingdom. Go your ways, bid the people be of good cheer, for the young King desireth not the hurt of any, but he desireth that the people be prosperous and happy. I desire that no one be hurt for cleaving to my uncle, the late King, let every man go forth to his labour, and be content, then will our land be prosperous and will our people be happy. Let the High Priest now go in and make offerings for the people.

[*Trumpets sound and scene closes.*]

### SCENE 2ND.

[*Outside the city, on the holy mountain of Gheba. The body of Protilahan lying in a coffin. Selsus seated in sackcloth beside it. Two others of the friends of the dead King with him. Time, night.*]

SELSUS.—A mighty man this day hath fallen on the earth. The sun hasteth to go down, and the moon hideth her face in darkness, for lo, a great light hath gone out. In the King's seat are scoffers, traitors and murderers. How hath the mighty this day fallen.

SOLDIER [*to other soldiers aside*].—Have yet the eagles come ? My bones tremble within me. My soul is devoured with trembling.

SECOND SOLDIER [*aside*].—What meanest thou by eagles ?

FIRST SOLDIER.—Knowest thou not that the carcass of a murderer, or a false-hearted man, if lain here as is the custom, the eagles will come and pluck out the eyes of the body, so that that soul shall for ever grope in darkness, throughout the lower pit. Ah ! my heart quaketh. Methinks I hear them coming.

SECOND SOLDIER [*aside*].—Fool, cease thy prating. Dost thou desire to vex the good Selsus with thy old hags' tales. Rather keep thy peace, and trouble not the great general.

FIRST SOLDIER.—Ah, friend, but why is the dead placed on this mountain. Is it to know if they will go to the land of the good spirits, or to the land of the bad ? Thou knowest that

the King did much wrong.  Ah ! hark !  I heard the sound of
their wings.  I am as a dead man.  They come !

SECOND SOLDIER.—'Tis naught but thy foolish coward
heart.  Thou had'st better cast away thy weapons of war and
spin with the women.  Away !  Leave, if thou can'st not be
quiet.

[SELSUS *speaks.*]

SELSUS.—O, treason.  O, treachery.  O, perfidy.  Thy
names are Saber and Ackbah and El Kohath.  They seemed
to love the King, and secretly encompassed his death.  While
they bowed before him their hearts plotted destruction to his
kingdom.  And now since he is dead the soldiers and chief
men bow down to the traitorous wretch, who was nurtured by
thee, O, Protilahan.  May the blood dry within me, may sleep
forever depart from me, if ever I bow down to the false King,
whom this day they made King.

[*Some one approacheth.*]

[*Enter* ACKBAH.]

FIRST SOLDIER.—Hist !  Ah, the eagles come.  [*He is terrified.*]

ACKBAH.—Peace friends.  Good Selsus, we were once
friends.  I come to do a friendly act, and watch with thee beside the body of the King.

SELSUS.—Hence, away !  Defile not the sacred presence of
the great King's body, by *thy* presence.  Thou art a two-faced
traitor, and while seeming to be a devoted slave of the King
did secretly plot his ruin.  I spit upon thee !  And, hear,
Ackbah, though it gorgeth me to speak thy name—tell thy
creature Saber, that sooner than bow down to him, would I
be thrown into the pit of boiling pitch.  And further, say to
him that while life lasteth I will hate him, and while Selsus
hath strength to lift weapon will he war against thy whole
murderous crew.  Leave my sight.

ACKBAH.—Selsus, thou art distempered by the events of
the few days past.  When thou art calm thou wilt be sorry
for thy words.  I hold thee not to account for thy conversation ; I only come to do thee friendly office.  [*He goes.*]

FIRST SOLDIER [*in terror*].—Ah ! they come.  The eagles !

[*Scene closes*].

## Scene 3rd.

[*In the King's palace. The young king alone. He talks.*]

Kuros.—And is this the height of greatness? Is it to have supreme power over the great land, and the only true pleasure rudely torn from me. Just now hath the physician told me of Althea. O, calamity most dire; were she dead, then could I mourn for her, and be reconciled, for we must submit to the decrees of fate. But she is here, in this great city, and separated from me by a most accursed custom. I loathe the brood of priests and priestesses, with their bloody laws and vain whims. This maiden thinketh that her vow bindeth her for ever. I must speak with good El Kohath. [*He calls.*]

[*Enter* Naroth, *Lord Chamberlain, prostrating himself.*]

Kuros.—Good Naroth, call El Kohath my trusty physician.

[El Kohath *appears.* Naroth *retires.*]

El Kohath.—Mighty King, what is thy wish?

Kuros.—Thou did'st startle me, I knew not of thy presence.

El Kohath.—I heard thy conversation, and know what is on thy mind. This is a most vexed question. I know not what to do. According to the laws of the Priesthood, a man cannot enter the Temple of the Vestal Virgins. Not even thee, O King. I have a plan in mind : Let Maida, the mother of Althea, visit the temple, and see the Priestess in thy behalf. Like thee, I have little temper with this priestcraft. 'Tis much delusion, much blind belief, some mystery and all useless. But trust me, noble King, and we will see what may be done. I go to seek Maida. [*He goes.*]

## Scene 4th.

[*In the Temple of the Vestal Virgins. High Priestess at her devotions. Other virgins around. Enter female porter of the Temple.*

Porter·—Most holy Priestess, a woman in the outer court would speak to thee.

High Priestess.—Let her be admitted. It is one of the world's people who is in distress. Let us ever be ready to minister unto such as are in need, for so commandeth our holy religion.

[*Enter* Maida.]

MAIDA.—Noble and sacred Priestess, forgive the presumption of my entering unbidden in thy presence.

[*Bows in Oriental fashion.*]

HIGH PRIESTESS.—Speak sister, what is the need that brings thee here?

MAIDA.—Most Holy Priestess, it is the woes of a mother that brings me here.

HIGH PRIESTESS.—Our mission is to relieve, as far as within us lies, the misery of our fellows.

MAIDA.—Ah! would that all misery were as easily relieved as mine. I have a darling daughter who is in the sacred Temple of the Vestal Virgins.

HIGH PRIESTESS.—Thou art then a happy mother. Thy daughter is dead to thee, but is living a new life of noble self-sacrifice, of good deeds, and of chaste honour. Thy daughter is no more to thee now than if she were already buried beneath yonder holy mountain.

MAIDA.—But, noble Priestess, she came here under a misapprehension. She deemed one dead who was all of her earthly life, and under the first blow of so dire a calamity she entered this life. The one supposed to be dead still liveth, and is lately crowned King of Gheba.

HIGH PRIESTESS.—Woman, I may not babble with thee, for all this talk is vain babbling. If thou hast no other grievance, go thy ways, for it is as impossible for thy daughter to go hence and renounce her vows, as for one to rise from the dead. Depart and trouble us no more.

[MAIDA *goes, weeping.*]

HIGH PRIESTESS.—Let every one go to her duties, and call Althea, our newly-made sister.

[*All go out, and* ALTHEA *enters.*]

HIGH PRIESTESS.—Sister, see that thou attend strictly to thy duties if thou would'st be perfectly happy when life is over. Hear nothing from this outside world; listen to no news; believe nought thou should'st hear. Forget the world if thou would'st be happy.

ALTHEA.—Ah, noble mother, I am slow to learn to crush every feeling that maketh life worth living. It seemeth a hard thing that all that is pleasant to the human heart should be plucked out as something wrong and vicious.

HIGH PRIESTESS.—Thou must rid thyself of such thoughts and feelings. They are natural to the lower instincts of man, and savour not of the higher and better part of him. Lay aside the evil part of thy nature, and prepare thyself for the joys of a holy and unchangingly happy life beyond this. Oh! 'tis noble to deny one's self, to conquer the grosser animal nature, and to live holy and chastely, and serve the poor and suffering of our kind. Oh, my sister! think ye well of these things.

ALTHEA (*weeping*).—Holy mother, I will try to the best of my ability; but my very nature revolteth against it.

HIGH PRIESTESS.—Then will there be more honour and worthiness in overcoming thy natural propensities. Come—let us go and perform our devotions, and listen to the voice of the sacred Oracle.

[*They go and kneel before the altar.*]

HIGH PRIESTESS.—O most sacred Oracle, what sayest thou?

VOICE (*from behind the altar*).—Hear, ye mortals. It is better to live nobly your natural lives, than to try to live an unnatural holy life.

[HIGH PRIESTESS *alarmed.* ALTHEA *flees.*]

·VOICE [*to* HIGH PRIESTESS].—·Woman, thinkest thou to crush out the life from these young hearts, by fastings and prayers. Nay. Thou are doing a great wrong. Bid the maiden Althea return to her mother and to her holier, happier life of a bride to her chosen husband.

HIGH PRIESTESS.—Nay, nay. It must not be [*aside*]. But I ne'er heard the Oracle so plainly.

[*She flees in terror.* ELKOHATH *comes from behind the curtain, and goes out unperceived.*]

### SCENE 5TH.

[*In the* KING'S *apartment,* KING, EL KOHATH *and others present.*]

KING.—Good physician, tell us of thy visit to the Temple of the Virgins and what thou did'st see there, for my soul burneth with impatience.

EL KOHATH.—I went unto the temple, and easily entered therein. I secreted myself in the curtains behind the altar for they are not disturbed save four times a year. I saw the mother of the maid enter, and I heard her repulsed. I afterwards heard the High Priestess plead with the maiden, for Althea taketh not kindly to that life. I afterwards spoke to the priestess and maiden by voice of their Oracle, which I knew filled the High Priestess with terror. But she can not let the maiden go, and I cannot see myself, any way out of this difficult matter.

KING.—I will have this maiden out of this vestal temple if I go and utterly destroy it : I will fetch her out, though I ride in on my good war-horse and take her by force. But stay, let us call the good Zorotus. He hath a mind ripened by long years of intelligent experience. Bid him come.

*Interval.—[Chamberlain heralds approach of* ZOROTUS *[he enters.]*

ZOROTUS.—Most worthy and noble King.

KING.—Venerable father, prostrate not thyself unto me. Rather would I prostrate unto thee. For there is no excellence save that of wisdom and honour, and both thou possessest to the fullest. But father, we desire thy advice in a most difficult and troublesome matter. Thou understandest how that Althea, my betrothed, had joined herself unto the Vestal Virgins.

ZOROTUS.—Yea, noble youth, I understand fully. It is a most sad affair. This vow is one of the most binding of our religion, and but one way remaineth to overcome it.

KING.—Speak, Holy Priest, how one way remaineth.

ZOROTUS.—That, likewise, is most difficult, and must have the maiden's consent thereto. It is this : She must to all appearance die, then be dressed for burial, and be exposed on the holy mountain, as is the custom, for three days. Then must she be lowered into the tomb and raised : then is the oath of no effect, and she becometh as she was before. But I know the High Priestess, and know she would never consent to have the maiden renounce her vows. Noble youth, it is impossible to recover the maiden.

KING.—Nay, good Zorotus, I will reclaim her, though I die.

ZOROTUS.—Son, do naught rash or hasty, nor aught to bring

reproach on thee, if thou defilest the sacred Temple of the Virgins. Beware the curse of the consecrated.

[*He goes out.*]

EL KOHATH.—Noble King, I know how thou canst reclaim the maiden from the vestal temple. I will show thee hereafter.

[*Scene closes.*]

## PART SIXTH.

### SCENE 1ST.

[*In the temple of the Vestal Virgins. Enter* ALTHEA *alone. She kneels before the altar. She communes with herself.*]

ALTHEA.—My soul is filled with horror of this holy place, for when the Oracle spake yesterday unto the Priestess, she was filled with fear. Yet methought the voice was that of El Kohath. It was a fancy, for the holy Oracle speaketh not by men's mouths. But with all my terror I must speak to the Oracle if Saber was murdered by the King. Most holy Oracle, thou knowest.

VOICE (*solemnly*).—Thy lover is not dead, but liveth, and pineth for thee. Go thou and seek him.

ALTHEA.—O, sacred temple! it is Saber's voice.

[KING, *in disguise, rushes out and catches her up.* HIGH PRIESTESS *and other* PRIESTESSES *hear the voice and enter. They are in terror, but attempt to keep him from bearing her off; but he rushes through with the unconscious maiden, and bears her away. Great noise among the virgins.* · *Scene closes.*]

### SCENE 2ND.

[*On the holy mountain of Gheba again. Time, night,* MAIDA *and the* KING (*in disguise*) *watching by a coffin.*]

KUROS.—Good mother, to-morrow breaketh our vigil, and we have not tasted food nor water these three days, that our loving watch may be like hers. O, that I might fast and watch yet other days to show my love for thee, most precious daughter of the ancient Kings of Gheba. Thou shalt sit beside me on the ancient throne of Gheba, and there will not be in all the land one so fair, or one so good as thou. And, I will decree that no more a maiden entereth the walls of the Temple of the Vestal Virgins, or ever shall a young man be compelled to join the priesthood of the Fire Worshipers.

### LAST SCENE.

#### *Tableau.*

[KING KUROS *stands before the throne of Gheba, the royal crown and the vestments of the Kings of Gheba upon him. By his side, clasping his hands, stands* ALTHEA, *clad in the royal robes also. In front, upon the sacred altar, burns the holy fire.* ZOROTUS, *the chief priest, stands before it, facing the King and Queen with hands spread over them, apparently blessing them. Grouped around stand the nobles and great men of Gheba, in the robes of the nobility of Gheba. Slow music outside. Curtain slowly falls.*

# DERMOT M<sup>c</sup>MURROUGH

𝔄 𝔇rama.

(TIME, A. D. 800.)

"PROSPECTOR" PRINT.
DEL NORTE,
COLORADO.

1882.

# DERMOT McMURROUGH.

## A Drama.

### TIME, A. D. 800.

———•◆•———

PERSONS REPRESENTED :

DERMOT MCMURROUGH.—King of Ireland.
BRIAN.—Brother of the King.
ARMAGH.—Chief Man-at-Arms.
HUGH.—A Trusty Servant.
BALLYNOOK.—Chief of Outlaws.
STEPHEN.—Son of Ballynook.
NORA.—Daughter of Ballynook.
DENNIS.—Chief Forester.
REDBEARD.—An Outlaw.
OLD MAN.—A Priest.
MCNAGNISH and FITZWILLIAM.—King's Officers.
TEAGUE of LEATH.—A Chief.
FAHERTY.—A Boatman.

Robbers, Soldiers, &c.

ETHELRED.—King of Britain.
EDGAR.—Brother of the King.
ESTELLA.—Sister of the King.
ANDELWALD.—A Courtier.
HARPER.—A Cambrian.

———

# DERMOT McMURROUGH.

## 𝔄 𝔇𝔯𝔞𝔪𝔞.

———◆———

## PART FIRST.

SCENE 1ST.—[*Dermot McMurrough, the King of Ireland, discovered in his great audience hall, Courtiers, Soldiers and others surrounding him. Time, A. D. 800.*]

McMURROUGH.—Ho, there, bloody villains! where is Armagh, my trusty man-at-arms, my worthy Captain. Speak, or by the powers of the air I'll hang the last villain of ye.

DENNIS [*The Chief Forrester coming forward*].—Your Majesty we know not. Behold we are inferior officers to the mighty Armagh, and we can control not his coming or going for he goeth where it pleaseth him, and no man can bid him save yourself, the mighty ruler of Ireland.

KING.—Dennis, were it not for thy usefulness I would cause a merry-making for the rabble to-morrow, by having thee hanged for thy presumption. However, I must e'en disappoint the people, and do myself an injustice by allowing thee to live on a little space. But hear me Dennis, and ye all, ye grinning rabble, unless tidings are brought me of the whereabouts of Armagh by night fall, it were better that ye hang yourselves in a bunch with your bow strings. Depart from me. [*They all go out leaving* McMURROUGH *alone.*]

KING [*Solus*].—There they go, as worthless a lot of grinning vagabonds as ever King was cursed with. Ah! that I had a thousand men, like the valiant Armagh. Then would I gladly join issue with the proud Briton beyond the sea. But there is not the likes of Armagh within the bounds of the world, mighty in stature, noble and brave in mind, he is alone in his excellence, I would he were here. Hist, what is that!

[*A bugle sounds.   Enter* ARMAGH.]
By the spade of Philla McCool.   There he comes.

KING.—Ah, ye rogue, sure, ye have murdered me with watching for ye to come, where hast thou been, good Armagh ?

ARMAGH.—Good sovereign, I have but been to my cottage beyond the heath, where thou knowest I grow the provender to keep this life in me.   Did I not tell thee ? then do I ask thy forgiveness.

KING.—Nonsense, 'tis a matter of no moment.   But I have longed to talk with thee, away from this stupid rabble, whose best purpose would be to hang from time to time to amuse my loyal subjects.   And whilst I speak of it, Armagh, do thou at thy convenience seek me stout any serviceable men, men of likely appearance, to stand in my house, and turn these gaping heathens adrift, sure, I am ashamed that visitors to my dominions should see them stalking around like ghosts of worn-out beggars.   Better that they till the soil, and each one produce his measure of oatmeal and peas.

ARMAGH.—Thou hast well said, good sovereign, they are truly an unlikely lot, yet within each rough and homely breast beats a true heart for thee and Old Ireland.

KING.—Armagh, I ask thy pardon.   Thou art right.   The men are true and valiant and their shabbiess of manner is more my sin than theirs.   I would not part with one of them for half the army of the Northmen.   Nay, Armagh, dismiss not one of them but rather do thou order from my weavers good strong cloth and the best and warmest of sheep skins, and let them be properly clad and armed.   Well, this is matter of very light import.   Hast thou heard of the movements of the Saxon King, the fair haired boy of Britain ? Odds Kings ! but I am minded to dismiss my soldiers, throw my spear and bow into the bog, and go tend sheep with the women, when I think of such as he being King.   Bad luck to me were there none other such, would I have the royal sport driving them into the sea with an old hag's besom.

ARMAGH.—Worthy Sovereign, Ethelred is indeed but a fair-haired lad, with a soft hand to woo blushing maidens withal, yet thou knowest that many a strong and valiant arm would be lifted for him, and many a stout heart's best blood would be poured out ere harm came to him.   Whoso meeteth the Saxon army hath need of strong bows and heavy axes, and many a good brawny arm to wield them. Yea, Dermot McMurrough, thou knowest that no one can stand before them, since the stout Dane hath thrice been driven back from the shores of Albion.

KING.—Armagh, thou speakest the born Briton. Sure but I have been mistaken all this time, and thou art one of the mighty Ethelred's born subjects. Och, but mayhaps I am speaking to the ambassador of Briton's King.

ARMAGH.—O King, thou hast a sovereign right to speak as thou seemest best to thy thanes. Laugh at me as thou wilt. Yet when Old Ireland or Dermot McMurrough has need of the heart's blood of Armagh, then will it flow as freely as water down a hill. Yea, though I love Britain, yet would I help carry fire and sword throughout her borders before harm should come to thee, or aught but peace and happiness should come to thy kingdom.

KING.—Armagh, thou art always right. Peace, I did but jest with thee. Sure but I know that a truer heart than thine does not beat. Thou hast my love and confidence. Thou truly art a born Briton, but thou art by instinct and nativity one of my truest subjects. Let us speak now more seriously. Thou didst speak to me of the lovely sister of the Briton King. I have long been pondering of thy words concerning her, until my sleep is disturbed by visions of her golden hair, flowing over the arched marble of her shoulders. Armagh, she is a being of more than earthly beauty. Of that I am convinced. Now, what I would speak to thee is this : I am enamoured of this Saxon Princess, and I command thee to go forth and seek her hand in marriage for me. Thou hast lately been to the Saxon Court. Thou knowest the speech and customs of that people. Thou canst command in my name the boatmen trading to those shores, or anything in my kingdom necessary to perform thy mission. Make ready and go without delay. [KING *arises and goes out.*]

ARMAGH.—Alas, my master thinketh not that he is a wild barbarian, and his kingdom well-nigh a wilderness. What would the gentle Estella think to see him and his palace ? It was a luckless day that I ever spake to him of her. What shall I do ? I must e'en obey him. Though gentle and kind as he

now is to me, he can be the wild murdering savage if I refuse
to obey him. Not that I fear him. Far from it. And when
I return with her refusal, which I do not for an instant doubt
she will give, who can curb his anger? Well, so may it be. I
will return to Ethelred's Court, and e'en attempt this wooing;
but methinks the King of Britain will at least take my life for
such presumption. [*He goes out.*]

SCENE 2ND.—[*In the forest, near Dublin.* BALLYNOOK, *the
outlaw, with* REDBEARD, STEPHEN *and* DENNIS, *the King's
Forester.*

BALLYNOOK.—What said'st thou, good Dennis? Did the
King command Armagh to go and woo the Saxon Princess for
him?

DENNIS.—He did. I heard it myself from behind the area.

BALLYNOOK.—Ha! ha! As well mightest thou mate the
roaring bull with the gentle fawn of the forest. Dost McMurrough think that the lady would permit him to groom her
horses? Were I not so deeply engaged in our most honourable business of relieving the overburdened wealth of the road,
I would e'en advance Armagh, and woo the lass with better
success myself.

REDBEARD.—A murrain take thee and all the Saxon women,
and men and children, for that matter. Yea, and evil fall on
these peaceful marrying times, when an honest man hath not
chance for a livelihood, except a beggarly penny from some
wandering miser. Nay, give me war, and plenty of it—blood
too, I say; then will the Flemish gold jingle in our hands, instead of this rusty copper. A shrewd and cutting life for me.

DENNIS.—A shrewd life it would be for thee, and a short
one, if Dermot McMurrough's men would overtake thee.

REDBEARD [*drawing his sword*].—Villain! what am I but what
thou art; what art thou that I am not? A vile traitor, who
eats bread of the man whom he deceives. A skulking robber,
who hath not the grace to cleave to the forest, but seemeth to
be an honest man. Ye murdering vagabond, draw!

[DENNIS *draws his sword.* BALLYNOOK *rushes between them.*]

BALLYNOOK.—Peace, lads. Save thy swords for common
foes. There will be occasion for their use, when Dennis and
Redbeard can fight side by side. Ye are both in the same
peril, and in the same business. Dennis, thou art useful to us,

being in the King's household ; and thou, my valiant Redbeard, thou art to me as the staff to declining age, or the harp to the ancient minstrel. Put away thy swords and let them not be drawn, save on occasion of common peril. He did but speak in jesting mood. Henceforth, Dennis, curb thy sharpened tongue ; and thou, Redbeard, hold thy fiery temper, that like an unmanageable horse, breaks away from thee. We know our common peril. Small luck would it be to any of us for the henchman of McMurrough to lay hands upon us. Redbeard, wilt thou depart to our place of meeting, and bid our men be wakeful and sleep as doth the hare when the crafty fox lieth upon her trail. Sharp work is ahead, and strong, active arms are needed. Bid all be ready ere the bannock cock croweth. Go in haste and peace, good Redbeard ; and thou, gentle Stephen, bear him company. [*They go out.*]

DENNIS.—I thought to be devoured entirely.

BALLYNOOK.—I tell thee, Dennis, it is well that thy head is not broken, asking pardon of thy valour. A gentler man than Redbeard might have cracked thy skull. What a passion thou kindlest in him ! But he is no secret enemy. Steenie maketh a good foil for Redbeard. He can vent his spleen upon him freely, and it hath no more effect than wine upon a post.

DENNIS.—Well, I fear him not, nor any such blusterer. But how cometh that mewling idiot in the ranks ? I often thought to ask thee.

BALLYNOOK.—Dennis, thou knowest not how thou speakest, or I would smite thee for it. Be more guarded in thy speech, or I will not answer for thy safety. Seek not to know what concerns thee not. Stephen may have a weak mind, but he knoweth better when and how to speak than many who claim greater wit. He is faithful and trustworthy, let that be sufficient for thee. And now, thou sayest that Armagh goeth to Britain with presents and offerings for the Princess. Small good may they do her. Were it any other man in Ireland who bore them than Armagh, they would go to enrich our merry band. Surely I fear not but we could take them, but a more valiant hearted man ne'er trod brake or glen than Armagh. Many of our good men would go down, before the treasure would be ours, and then we would be compelled to slay him before we could lay hands upon them. And I tell thee, Dennis, our country can ill spare such as Armagh. I freely tell thee, I love plunder, and our free greenwood life, yet I love old Erin much more. In Armagh I see the hope of our benighted and darkened land. I tell thee further, that it is much less to be a robber here where all are robbers, than in more favoured lands. Was I not driven from my home and kindred by the oppressions of that brutal savage, Dermot Mc-Murrough. Bad luck to his black visage. It would better ornament the top of a robber's post, than any of ours. I would that Armagh were now King, then would there be no more loyal or honest man between the two seas, than Ballynook. But, good Dennis, knowest thou not of some fairer plunder than the presents that Armagh beareth to the Prin-cess ?

DENNIS.—Nay; what better plunder want'st thou than that ? Sure, all the best jewels and gold and the likes, goeth with Armagh.

BALLYNOOK—By the holy cudgel, I will not harm a penny that Armagh guardeth, and woe be it to any of Ballynook's men who trieth it.

DENNIS—So let it be, I but did my duty to thee, and that at the risk of my own life. I will make what shift possible back to the castle. Fair and hearty, good captain. [*He goes.*]

BALLYNOOK—There he goes, to smile and fawn upon the man he is betraying. But who knoweth that the villain will not betray me. Dost not the fox carry provender back and forth ? I will e'en set a strict watch upon him, and at the first sign of treachery he will walk the dark bog of Kilkleuch. The fiends fly off with the smooth face upon him. The best luck I wish him is to have the gentle McMurrough get his anger kindled against him. But I must away to the robbers' tryst.

[*He goes.*]

SCENE 3RD—*In the robbers' glen, deep in the forest. Time, night.* BALLYNOOK, REDBEARD, STEPHEN, CRASSIE, *and other Robbers around, all armed with the weapons of the time.* BALLYNOOK *arrayed in garments made of wolf-skins, his head ornamented with a cap made of the skin of the wolf's head.*

BALLYNOOK—How sayest thou, lads, hath yet the wild wolf bayed ?

STEPHEN *(singing)*—

The wild wolf bays, the forest rings,
The owl's abroad, the night-bird sings,
The traveller hastes him on the road,
Come, come, my lads, we must abroad.

[*All join in chorus.*]

Ho, Ho, the robber O,
A merry life for me.
While others love the bounding wave,
Give us the forest free.

[*Chorus repeated.*]

BALLYNOOK—My trusty men, ye know how that Armagh goeth to Britain, with treasure of the King's house. No one doubteth that we could fetch it away, yet not a hair of Armagh's head shall fall by any act of Ballynook's men. I shall cause anyone who disobeys this command to be slain, and his head placed upon a pole in this forest. Do ye all hear that ?

REDBEARD—How now. Why hath the valiant captain come to so tame a conclusion ? Methinks he cannot fear even so valiant a man as Armagh.

BALLYNOOK—Hold thy peace. Thou full well knowest that I fear not any man. Thou likewise remembereth that our country hath no more faithful son than Armagh. Did not we fight beside him on the Black Moor. Shame on thee, Redbeard.

REDBEARD—Thou art right. I will not molest Armagh, and death to him that doth. But, hist ! Here cometh the short-eared wolf, the crafty fox. [*Enter* DENNIS.]

BALLYNOOK—Welcome Dennis. Thou'rt late, but still seasonable. What tidings bringest thou, my merry son of war.

DENNIS—Sure, but I got away just in time, Armagh goeth to the sea-coast but to-morrow, with the king's jewels that ye mind were taken at the fight with the Flemish at the Black Moor. In troth, better salvage hath never fallen into thy hands, for he is attended by a beggar's crew who will flee like hares at the first jingle of our swords, and what is one man's valour against forty, even if he be the great and valiant Armagh.

BALLYNOOK—I told thee, Dennis, that no harm should come to Armagh nor the treasure that he guardeth. Sure, if he wanted escort and protection, my trusty lads would give it him. What say you ?

ALL.—We would, noble Ballynook.

DENNIS.—Then if thou fearest the great Armagh, and thy band of honest gentlemen are over scrupulous about taking the treasure, I must e'en seek worse company.

REDBEARD.—When thou sayest that we fear aught, villain, thou liest ! [DENNIS *flings a javelin at* REDBEARD, *which misses him and strikes* STEPHEN, *mortally wounding him,* DENNIS *escapes in the darkness.* BALLYNOOK *rushes to the lad and raises him, makes lamentations.*]

BALLYNOOK.—O the villain ! He has slain my own son. O my boy ! Speak to your father. Men, pursue the bloody murderer. Let him not escape the forest. My poor bairn, can'st thou not look at thy father ?

STEPHEN [*feebly*].—Ah, the mist and fog that hath settled into the forest. Sure, but I can't see a hand's breadth. It is cold, too, and there is no coat upon me to keep me warm. Father, father, where art thou ?

BALLYNOOK.—Here, here, my lad, I am beside thee. See'st thou me ?

STEPHEN.—Alas ! All are gone and I am alone. The forest is dark and cold and I perish. Ah ! It is lighter, the mist and fog is rising, and I begin to see light among the trees, I am warmer too. See how beautiful the light. O the beautiful music. It is light and warm now. [*He dies.*] [BALLYNOOK *makes great lamentation while all leave in search of* DENNIS, *save* REDBEARD *and* CRASSIE.]

REDBEARD.—Good Crassie, this night must that traitorous wretch be taken before he reaches the King's castle. He will betray the matter to the King and to Armagh. McMurrough hath large force wherewith to scour the forest, and drive us to the sea. Thou art fleet of foot, Crassie. Thou knowest the road he will take to return, go thou quickly through to the four oaks by the King's highway, and smite him dead, and I will give thee the jewel-hilted dagger I had from the King of Ireland. Go quickly. [*Crassie goes.*]

REDBEARD [*to* BALLYNOOK].—Master. It was my rashness that caused the lad's death. Smite me and let me die.

BALLYNOOK.—Nay. Nay, my trusty friend. Trouble not thy mind, but rather go thou and secure the cowardly murderer.

REDBEARD.—Rather permit me to wait with thee, for this chase is now far from here, and all our good men pursue him.

BALLYNOOK.—Good friend, at this sore time, it doeth me great good to have thy presence. O, my poor harmless boy. O, Steenie, my bairn. [*He weeps.* REDBEARD *wraps a mantle over the body.*]

SCENE 4TH.—[*In the King's council room, a rude interior, ornamented with old weapons, armour, antlers, flitches of bacon, sausages, &c.* KING *and* ARMAGH.]

McMURROUGH.—Now, my noble Armagh, what thinkest thou of thy mission. The lady will be highly pleased, sure, to have the chance of getting so fine a looking husband as myself. Besides, am I not the ruler of the largest part of this delightful kingdom, and have I not conquered all of these petty chiefs, barring the Chief Teague of Leath, bad sight to his bloody eyes, but I'll have him after ye return. The princess will require but short time to make up her mind. Ah! Armagh, but it's the fine feast we will have when ye return. Sure, but I will wish I had such a forester as Ballynook again, may the dragons crawl off with him, then would I have such dainty meats of the forest as we scarce see in these times. But now the rascally outlaws eat the best, and my hunters get only the old and crippled deer. Ah! But here comes Dennis. Speak knave, why comest thou in without giving warning? [*Enter* DENNIS. *out of breath running.* DENNIS *attempts to speak*]

KING.—Ah, ye rogue, but I will e'en shake ye more than that if thou stand gaping at me like a sick cat. Speak out man, what aileth thee?

DENNIS [*with difficulty*].—Sure, as I was coming through the forest to-night I saw a great light, and going there to find what was the matter, your majesty, I found it was the grand meeting place of the outlaws, and they set upon me, and I slew one with my spear, when I ran away from them, and out-ran them until I came to the four oaks by the highway, when a murdering thief who was behind cast a spear at me, and had I not happened to stumble, sure he would have killed me entirely, as it was, he has cut me in the back, you can see.

KING.—So he did, and bad luck to him for his poor aim. Go thy ways, Dennis, and let the priest of the oak leech thy back. [*Dennis goes out.*] Armagh, we must to-night go forth with trusty men and scour the forest. These villains must be captnred at any risk. By the holy giant but it will be a grand frolic to hang the lot of them on my wedding day. Sure, but I think that Ballynook is at the head of the gang. But I long to lay my hands upon him.

ARMAGH.—It is a great pity that so brave a man should be in such company. Knowest thou not that at the battle of the Black Moor, none fought so valiantly, and none with such effect as Ballynook.

KING.—So the wild boar of the forest is brave, and the wolf fighteth for her den, but we slay them, likewise, when we have opportunity. How many men can we bring together?

ARMAGH.—Above forty, by midnight, your Majesty.

KING.—Then will I seek my couch, and do thou make ready, take the men, with Dennis to show the way.

ARMAGH.—But suppose there is danger to Dennis to take him out with such a wound?

KING.—Fear not. He has been born for a merrier death than that. Yea, and a drier one. I shall hang the villain with the rest, for I am of the opinion that he belongeth to the band, and hath had some quarrel with them, and in revenge hath reported this story. Make ready, good Armagh, and lose no time. I would go forth myself, when all is ready. [*They go out. Dennis appears from behind. He shows the greatest terror.*]

DENNIS [*speaking to himself.*]—Ah, the King knoweth my secret. Where shall I hide my guilty head? I cannot go back to the outlaws, and I cannot escape to Teague by reason of my wound. I will e'en go forth, and show Armagh the place, and haply I may get favour with McMurrough. I will e'en live an honest life, if I can but escape this great danger, An honester, truer-hearted man shall not be found in all Ireland, if I but save myself from this pine. Oh, that I had but remained in my cottage, and not sought honour from the King. Ha, there comes the Captain, [*He sneaks out.* ARMAGH *enters, speaking to himself.*]

ARMAGH.—So the King himself is minded to go out with the men. Oh! that I could turn him from this foolish purpose of wooing the Saxon maiden. It will come to naught, and he will blame me for the failure. Perhaps if we can get employment for his savage mind hunting the outlaws, he will forget it. But I shall be much grieved to see harm come to Ballynook, for a truer friend to his distracted country does not tread her soil. And I remember Redbeard quite well. Though he is rash and violent in his temper, yet his heart is in his hand for all good deeds to Erin. She needs such men. Even if they are outlaws, they were made so by the oppressions of McMurrough. Oh! that the day would come when all over the country would be prosperity, and peace, like the gentle sunshine, glow all over the green hills of Old Ireland. Fain would I lay down my life to bring quiet and peace to my country. And when the light of day should grow dim to my eyes, may I, the last sight I see, be the day star of brightness shining all over her borders. [*Noise outside. Enter* HUGH, *a good-natured attendant upon the King.*]

HUGH.—Ah, mighty Captain, a good night to your honour. Sure, but it is sorry the taste of sleep have I got the night, barring three or four hours. All for watching to speak with you concerning what the King wishes me to tell ye.

ARMAGH.—Well, honest Hugh, speak on, I am minding ye.

HUGH.—Well then, he said but just now, for I have been counting it on my fingers, so as not to forget, that ye shall take above forty good men. Do ye mind, Captain.

ARMAGH.—Yes, yes, go on.

HUGH.—Yes. He said you should take the men, and go out with Dennis, and capture the bloody thief that killed Dennis entirely. No, he said take Dennis, and lave the men, or lave Dennis, or wait until he comes out, and by the powers of darkness, but I don't mind which. Sure, but I have it now. He said for ye to take Dennis and wait with the men until he came out, for he can't sleep, for thinking of the jolly fight with the thieves.

ARMAGH.—I think, Hugh, that the loss of sleep hath upset thy mind. Better ye go and secure a little sleep, so ye can be in with the fight.

HUGH.—Troth, noble captain, but it is me mother's son that can't sleep while there is a prospect for a fight. Sure, but it is hard knocks I can be giving to the murdering outlaws. Let them come on me. Two or twenty, it is all one to Hugh.

*(He sings)* :

> Ah, give me a stick for every knave,
> And here's my hand to Paddie's brave,
> For jolly the fight we have to save
> Ould Erin from her foemen.
>
> For heads must crack, and blood shall spill,
> Ere yet we right the many ills,
> And clear Ould Erin from foemen.
>                 Whoop ! Hurrah !

ARMAGH.—Good Hugh, thy song is better, if possible, than thyself. But, do ye mind, that among these same outlaws is many a good friend to thy country. Sure, ye haven't forgotten who won the day down by Ballycleaugh. Now, Hugh, would ye be striking and killing so good a friend to Erin. Speak, man.

HUGH.—Sure, may the foul fiend fly off with me if I do. Wasn't it myself that stood beside him, when his good sword cut down through the armour of the Chief of Connaught, and sliced him like your honour would a leek. Then what a whoop he set up, that the whole force of vagabonds that followed him fled, as if all the demons of darkness were upon them. Bally-nook was the great man that day, and no one could stand before him. Sure, but it is myself that thinks that he was ill-treated.

ARMAGH.—Stop, stop, foolish fellow, dost mind who might hear thee ? Dost thy head sit so solid on thy shoulders that the broadsword cannot cut it off. If ye want to help right the ills of old Erin, that ye sing about, ye must e'en want to live, for dead men do no fighting.

HUGH—Ah, it is myself that wants to live anyhow, whether old Erin is righted or not.

ARMAGH.—Well, then, ye must keep a still tongue in that head of yours, if ye want it to sit nicely on your shoulders.

HUGH.—In faith, but I can keep as still as the first wake of McCool, the Irish Giant, where there was none to sit with the body but himself. Sure, but it is a long time they will wait for a wake if Hugh is to be the subject, and he brings the hanging on himself by talking. Bad luck to me, but who comes outside.                 [*Enter* McMURROUGH.]

McMURROUGH [*to* HUGH].—O, ye beastly bog-begotten villain, why did you not send me the Captain as I bid ye. Sure, but when I find time, I will hang ye for a common vagabond.

HUGH.—Great King, then may the saints keep ye busy for many a long year. May the snakes crawl off with me, but I was just telling the Captain how ye told me to tell him.

ARMAGH.—The fellow is not blameworthy, your majesty, as I was hearing his message when ye entered.

McMURROUGH.—Off with ye, then, lest a worse fate befall ye. Go to bed, and sleep, and see if ye can obey me now.

HUGH.—Sure, but it is many a harder task I have had. But little fear that I will disobey this time. [*He goes.*]

McMURROUGH.—Armagh, what is the time of night ?

ARMAGH.—It is now about the turn of midnight, for I hear e'en now the cocks crowing. [*Crowing outside.*]

McMURROUGH.—This night I hope to be revenged on my direst enemy. Ah, Ballynook ! I have thee by the throat. I tell thee, good Armagh, that there is not a pleasure in my life but is bittered by the thought that that villain still lives. And there is not a wish of my heart but would I throw away to have his heart's blood. Many is the curse I have heaped upon his head, and now I see the opportunity to tear him limb from limb. Sure, ye must not kill him outright even if ye have the chance, for I want the pleasure of tearing the eyes from his head while he yet lives. Armagh, get the men, and take that villain Dennis, and if he show us not the outlaws' camp, then will I treat him as I would the chief outlaw. Come, let us go.
[*They go out.*]

SCENE 5TH—[*In the Forest, at the trysting-place of the Outlaws.* BALLYNOOK *and* REDBEARD *sitting beside the body of* STEPHEN. *The body wrapped in a mantle,* BALLYNOOK *and* REDBEARD *moaning. Enter* NORAH, *the daughter of* BALLYNOOK, *and sister of* STEPHEN, *a vision of perfect female loveliness. She throws herself weeping on the ground by the body. Time, night.* BALLY-NOOK *speaks.*]

BALLYNOOK.—Good Redbeard. It is better that we have the body borne to the cottage beyond the burn, where once the dame resided. It is not meet that the lass be here in the forest, amid the damps of the night. Do thou go, then, to where the men are secreted, and fetch four trusty friends to make a bier of boughs, and bear my son to the cottage. Haste thee, good Redbeard, for it cometh on toward the midnight.
[REDBEARD *makes ready and goes forth.*]

NORAH.—O, woe is me. O, my brother, the companion of my youthful sports. So gentle, so kind, yet as brave as a warrior. O, how can I go on and live and thou dead. The spring shall come, then the summer, and the winter, and the years shall come and go, but thou, my brother, shall come among us no more. O, woe is me! O, my brother!

BALLYNOOK.—Oh! my boy. Thou wast the light of my life, the hope of my declining years, but my light has gone out in darkness and my hope is like the straw that has been cast into the oven. Oh, my son; that thou shouldst fall by the hand of a cowardly traitor, in the fulness of health and manhood. Oh, my poor bairn. [*He weeps. Noise of tramping of many feet. Rude orders given in the voice of* MCMURROUGH. *Enter* MCMURROUGH, ARMAGH, DENNIS *and men. Man with a torch comes forward.* MCMURROUGH *advances. He speaks.*]

MCMURROUGH.—Ha! thou thrice accursed wretch. Thou robber and murderer. Thou fiend of darkness. Thou curse of thy country. Now at last I have thee. O, but I will flay thee alive. I will pull thee limb from limb. Here, now, thou viper, and this thy demon's imp. Now will I have thy heart's blood. [NORAH *screams and throws herself on her father's neck.* BALLYNOOK *speaks.*]

BALLYNOOK [*to* McM.]—McMurrough, thou surely hast yet some heart of humanity in thee. Here lieth the dead body of my only son, and here is my defenceless daughter. Let me bury my son, even here with the help of thy men, and send my daughter away. They cannot harm thee. After that thou canst do with me as thou wilt.

MCMURROUGH.—Wretch, thou shalt die by inches, and this female whelp of thine shall see it, after which she shall be given to my soldiers. This vile carcass can be buried by the wild wolf. Ha! men; seize him. Armagh, take him. Villains, bind him. Let me tear out his eyes. Armagh, I command thee to seize him.

ARMAGH.—Never, while a drop of true Irish blood runs in my veins will I not touch a faithful son of old Ireland, nor shalt thou harm him while a breath remains in Armagh's body. [KING *grows furious; draws his sword; rushes at* BALLYNOOK. ARMAGH *with one blow of his cudgel knocks him senseless.* RED-BEARD *with attendants come up. Soldiers seeing the* KING *fall by*

ARMAGH'S *hand, scatter and retreat towards the castle taking the insensible* KING *with them.* NORAH *clings to her father.* REDBEARD *draws sword and makes toward* ARMAGH.]

BALLYNOOK.—Hold, good Redbeard. Noble Armagh, I thank thee to-night. Not that thou hast saved my life, for that is not worth the saving, but that thou hast raised thy hand in behalf of my defenceless child, and hast made it possible to give my dead bairn a human burial. Good Armagh, may heaven reward thee. I never can.

ARMAGH.—Ballynook, may the sun be forever dark to me, and may the blood dry in my veins, if I ever stand by and see a noble soul like thine tormented, or a fair lady like thy daughter suffer harm. No, no. Armagh wars not against grief-stricken hearts, nor defenceless women. Ballynook, let me mingle my tears with thine over the body of thy slain child, after which I will assist at the burial. For the present, I think it better that we remove the body of your son, and the young lady, to a place of greater safety. We well know the temper and the courage of McMurrough. He will be back by morning light, and I am with thee and thine, an outlaw to him. Let us not tempt his vengeance.

REDBEARD.—Noble sir, permit me to take thy hand. It is many a day since we met, and may it be a long day ere we part. See around thee thy slaves, thy born servants, who will spill the last drop of their blood in thy behalf, and in the behalf of our groaning country.

ARMAGH.—Good friend Redbeard, I am at the present time an outcast from my home and country. Alas, Armagh has no cause. But we must not idly talk here. Take thy men and remove the body of poor Steenie to a place of safety, and beg thy master to seek some sleep, for the night is far spent. So long as the lady and the grief-stricken father are in want of escort, just so long will I remain with thee. Henceforth my ways are beyond the borders of my country.

[*Men raise the body of* STEPHEN. NORAH *leans on the arm of her father, and all depart.*]

## PART SECOND.

SCENE 1ST.—[*In the King's house. Time near morning.* HUGH *alone walking the floor. He is displaying fear. Talks to himself.*]

HUGH.—O ! but it is a sorry day that I left the bogs and came to be a King's man. Sure it is the perfect gentleman I could have been, with my neat little cottage and my turf spade, and no trouble at all only to do me day's work and go home at night to me porridge and to me bed. Whisht, what is that. [*Cock crows outside.*] Bad luck to the throat of ye, for starting the life out of an honest man. But I wish it was morning, or else the King and the King's men would return. Sure every noise freezes the blood of me. Ha ! [*He looks around in terror.*] May the fiends fly off with the mice. I thought sure some one was coming. I feel to-night that there is great trouble and much blood being spilt. Sure when the King heard that Ballynook was to be captured, he looked like the wild beast when it is turned at bay in the forest. Sure but there is many good men and true behind Ballynook, and won't stand by and see him murdered. Oh it is no relish I have for fight, except it be a good natural bout with a bit of a blackthorn stick with a bosom friend. Stop now. What is that ? Some one comes. O by the holy hill of Howth. O saints of my grandfather defend me. O blood and murder. [*He falls on his knees in great terror, at the sight of the apparition that enters the door. Enter an old man with a long white beard, a white skull-cap on his head, and clad in a long black robe quite different from the half savage dress of the people. He speaks.*]

OLD MAN.— Son, why art thou overcome with fear ? I am come to Ireland to do good and not harm. I am thy friend, and the friend of thy people. I have come to call upon thy King, and to beseech him to turn from his ways and be no more a darkened heathen, and I come to teach the people of Ireland the knowledge of the truth.

HUGH.—O good Saint, come not near me, I mistrust thee.

[*He rises and retreats to the farther end of the room.*] Whist, go back, holy Priest, sure, I can talk quite well to thee at this distance, but if ye are on business elsewhere, I can readily excuse ye, and ye can depart. Ah, [*to himself*] but I am dead already with fear of him, with his long white beard ; sure but I think he comes from the other world.

PRIEST.—Why distrust me ; do I come with swords and cudgels to kill thee ? Shame on thee, man, for thy cowardice. See I am an old man in need of rest, for I trod from Craggie Head the night. Haven't ye a bit of bannock and a sup of milk, and a rug for a poor old man.

HUGH.—Now faith, he talks like a human, and he shames me indeed, for my fears. Good father, ye shall sup and sleep like a gentleman, and if thou lackest aught it will not be the fault of Hugh. Wilt thou sup or sleep first ?

PRIEST.—Good Hugh, I will sleep until the morning if thou wilt. Then will I break my fast with the dawning of the day.

HUGH.—Well then, holy father, pass through yonder portal, turn at the second door to thy right, when thou wilt find a bed sufficient for thee, good Priest that thou art. [PRIEST *blesses him and goes out.*]

HUGH.—Ah ! but it was the fright that the old Priest put in me. It is not pleasant that I feel yet at all. Who knows that he may not be after coming back and putting a spell on me. It is said that the Druid priests have the power to change a man into an ox, and how would I look with horns upon me, and switching a tail about me sides ? Ah, but it is bad luck to me. Hark ! O, by the powers of darkness, it is the old fiend himself that is coming this time. [*Noise of many feet outside. Murder and destruction. Enter soldiers bearing* KING *on a rude litter.*]

SOLDIER.—Fool, cease thy bawling, or by the cudgel of McCool I will knock the skull from thy shoulders. Dost thou not see that the King is wounded. Stir thyself and give what assistance thy muddled brain is capable of giving. [*They set the litter down.* KING *stirs. They assist him to rise.*]

MCMURROUGH.—O, the villains. My head is bursting. Send me Armagh. Come hither, Armagh. Armagh, thou art my right hand. Where is he ?

SOLDIER.—Your majesty, Armagh is not here. Wilt thou

be quiet, until we send for the Priest of the grove. Sure, he hath great skill to heal disorders, and thou hast been most foully dealt with. Easy, good King. Ah, may the good saints defend us. Who is yonder? [*Enter* PRIEST.]

PRIEST.—Peace be to thee, my friends, can I be of aid to the wounded man, I have some little skill in treating the wounds of the body. Let me see him. Good friend, let me examine thy wounds. [*He approaches the litter.*]

KING.—I am Dermot McMurrough. Sure no enemy hath ever got the better of me. Haven't I conquered and driven out all the chiefs except Teague of Leath, bad luck to him. And didn't I compel the vanquished Prince of Connaught to bring me food and water. Who said I was wounded? He lies. Sure no one hath the hardihood to strike me a blow in my own kingdom. Armagh come hither and disperse these vilains. [*He groans and lies down.*]

PRIEST.—Men, bring hither a basin, we must do somewhat for the King. I will bleed him, afterward he can sleep, then will he be better. [*They bleed him. Then all leave but* HUGH *and the* PRIEST.]

PRIEST.—Good Hugh, do thou watch beside him and I will retire again to the couch thou gavest me, I am in need of rest, but if he stirreth, call me. Dost thou understand?

HUGH.—I do, worthy father, may thy rest be easy. [PRIEST *goes out leaving* HUGH *with the wounded* KING. INTERVAL. KING *stirs, wakes up, looks around and calls* HUGH.]

McMURROUGH.—Where am I? Ha! Hugh is it thee, indeed. O! Saints of the stars defend me. My head is broken entirely. Good Hugh, come nearer, tell me what hath happened.

HUGH.—Your majesty, may the dragons crawl off with me if I can tell thee. Sure the soldiers brought ye back some time since with your head broken and lying as one dead on the litter. No one told me, but I suppose ye were wounded in the fight with the bloody outlaws.

McMURROUGH.—Ah! It all comes back to me, Hugh, my simple-hearted friend, I believe thee a true man. If I did not, I would not tell thee. It was no robber enemy that struck me. It was the man of all others that I trusted and leaned upon. It was Armagh. Hugh, there is treason in every breath of the wind. Sure there is murder behind every bush. The enemies of the King are in his house and sit beside him. Ah, but I will be avenged on the whole black-hearted lot. They are a band of murdering outlaws. I will take the field to-morrow. What is the time, good Hugh ?

HUGH.—Sure, your majesty, it must be near day, I but just now heard the morning crowing of the cocks, and the air feels fresh like the daybreak, and I see a lighter glow in the east.

KING.—Hugh, the good cause must not stand still, nor must I lie idly here, a single hour after the sun hath risen. Canst thou bring me a priest to leech my wounds.

HUGH.—Now may the saints be praised, sure there is one but here in the house. He stopped to crave a lodgment until the morning, with a sup of milk to start with when it is day. He is an old man and a venerable, I will bring him if it please your majesty. [HUGH *goes and presently returns with the venerable priest.*]

McMURROUGH [*In terror*].—Ah ! go away from me. Sure ye are the same one who haunted me but a little while ago in my dream.

PRIEST.—Noble King be easy in thy mind, I come with the best intent to do thee good. How can I assist thee.

McMURROUGH.—Venerable father, I ask thy pardon. As ye must see, I am but lately wounded, and my wits fly away with me. Good priest, I must be off to conquer and extermi-nate a vile band of outlaws, who distress my subjects, and create great terror throughout my dominions. Ah, but I must be well by the sunrise. Do thy utmost skill.

PRIEST.—Thou must rest. Here is a potion which will calm thy mind and cause thee to sleep. Thou art weak, but repose will bring thee strength.

McMURROUGH.—Hugh. Depart to thy repose [HUGH *goes out*]. Now venerable man, I would first speak to thee.

PRIEST.—No, your majesty must refrain from talking until thou sleepest. After which I hope to have a great deal of con-versation with thee.

McMURROUGH.—I will talk, I must have thy counsel, for I am impressed that thou art a good man, and a true Priest. There hath a band of outlaws infested my kingdom, as I told thee. That hath vexed me sore, for I could not find them to punish them. It was but yesterday that they assaulted and sorely wounded a faithful subject and a man of my household. But that is not the cause of my greatest vexation. At the head of this band is a man who is my bitterest enemy. Ah, but I could tear his heart from his breast. He hath crossed me in every way, and at the last has defied my authority, good father. I had beside me only yesterday, a man whom I loved more than any other. He was my support, my great reliance, and I could do nought without his counsel. Ah, the bitterness of destroyed confidence. It was his hand that struck me down to-night. When he should have stood by me, and fought for me to the death, he turned against me and smote me to the earth. O, but let me stand on my feet and I will gibbet the lot of them. They do not know Dermot McMurrough, or they would be ere this, embarking to leave Ireland forever. Ha, may the demons take the bloody crew, I will drive them into the sea.

PRIEST.—Peace, peace. Ye must be quiet if ye would stand upon your feet and be Dermot McMurrough again. Ye have fumed yourself into a fever. Take now this potion, and rest; then when thou art restored we will talk further. Take the draught. [PRIEST *gives him the draught, and he soon sleeps.*]

SCENE 2ND.—[*In the Forest near the Black Moor.* ARMAGH, BALLYNOOK, NORAH, REDBEARD, CRASSIE *and others present.*]

BALLYNOOK.—Armagh, in days gone by our country needed our best endeavours, and we fought side by side, with the same hopes and the same end in view. To-day our country groans under a tyrant more grinding than the one we fought. Let us make common cause, and help our countrymen throw off the usurper's yoke. Thou knowest, Armagh, that I have been a robber. I have taken by force. But what compelled me? Who drove me from home and kindred, for no reason only his jealousy of me? Last night he went down under thy good cudgel, and I only trust his head is thoroughly broken. Armagh, the people love and trust thee. There will be such a rising as hath not been seen since our fathers came over the sea. Only speak the word, and I will send trusty men throughout the land and rally the people. Ah, but they will come with a force that nothing will withstand them!

ARMAGH (*sadly*).—Ah, Ballynook, I cannot, I cannot bear

the name of traitor. I am broken in spirit, and do not wish to add to the woes of my distracted country by bringing on civil war. Peace under McMurrough, bad as he is, is better far than war. Oh let us not make our country groan with such a burden! Perhaps he will now do better. As for myself, I will go to Britain, where thou knowest I was born. This is my country, and when she is in sore need she shall have my services. I will go hence.

BALLYNOOK.—Good Armagh, it is thy presence at the Court that made McMurrough at all bearable. What will he do now? Kill, murder, and ravage the country, from one border to another. Thou art he alone that can bind the people together and make them as one man.

ARMAGH.—I think thou art wrong. I will go hence, and if I am needed I will return. It will be better thus. I have no time to spare, as McMurrough will be on the moor by the turn of the afternoon. I do not fear him, but it is better that I do not meet him. [*Enter* BALLYNOOK'S *men, dragging* DENNIS, *who is greatly terrified.*]

MAN.—Here, noble chief, knowest thou this man? We found him skulking in the forest. [DENNIS *throws himself on his knees.*]

BALLYNOOK.—Vile reptile! what mercy dost thou expect? Is it the same that thou gavest? Knowest thou that we have but just now buried mine only son, an innocent lad, that fell by thy hand? Decide thyself. Thou shalt be judge. What shall I do with thee?

DENNIS.—O noble Armagh! plead for me. I am wounded and broken. Good Ballynook, I aimed not to do thy son hurt. I would not have harmed a hair of his head. Thou knowest that it was an inadvertence. Oh let me live, if only to be the meanest servant!

BALLYNOOK.—Men, take him away for the present time. We will consider how to punish him, at some future time.

ARMAGH.—For my sake, strain thy mercy to its utmost in dealing with this fellow. He is no worse than his lord. He is the kind of a villain that McMurrough maketh of honest men. But I must away. Good Ballynook, whenever my country needs me I am ready to come. Thou knowest Faherty, the waterman. When I am needed here, give him this ring which

I now give thee, and tell him to bear it to me. He is a true man, and thou canst trust him. I must leave thee.

NORAH (*advancing and taking his hand*).—Noble Armagh, I cannot permit thee to leave until thou receivest the thanks of a homeless maiden for thy interposition in her behalf, and in behalf of her father, as I now can see, making thyself an outcast and an exile by so doing. Thy nobleness will ever be remembered by me, and wherever thou goest thou hast my heart with thee.

ARMAGH.—Gentle lady, I did but what any true-hearted man would have done. Thank me not, and cease to think of one whom life hath had the greenness destroyed from it as by fire, and whose heart is as the fallow field turned by the plough.

NORAH.—Ah! noble Sir, but the fallow field is sown and bringeth forth lustily again, and the once green meadow, swept by the fire will, erst while, grow green. O, Armagh, stay with us, and be the leader of the people as my father desireth thee.

ARMAGH.—Thou knowest not how thy words thrill me, but my resolution is taken, and I must hie me to Britain. It is better for our country that I should do so. But I take with me a tender remembrance of thee. Bear me kindly in mind, and hope as I do for a meeting in less stormy times.

NORAH.—Noble Sir, my heart is already thine, and if thou will't, I will go with thee and share thy exile.

ARMAGH.—It must not be. The danger is too great from the Northern robbers on the sea. Nay, gentle maiden, remain with thy father, and the female attendants whom I see with thee, and remember that Armagh has thee enshrined in his breast as his greatest treasure. [*Ballynook advances from rear.*]

BALLYNOOK.—My men desire that thou would'st pass judgment on this fellow Dennis. They will abide thy decision. Bring him. [*They bring* DENNIS *forward, who is cowering with terror.*]

ARMAGH.—We are men, and have hearts of men. This man is sore wounded. Let his wounds be dressed, and let him be made whole again. It is better to reclaim a bad man than to kill him. Perchance he will be a different tempered man henceforth. Spare him, if he shows himself worthy.

DENNIS.—O, noble Armagh, I thank thee for thy words, I am almost a dead man, but thou revivest hope in me. Truly will I be a better and more faithful man.

CRASSIE [*to his fellows*].—Ah, but it is bad luck to the aim I took at him. Odds, Faith, but I will do better next villain I throw at.

BALLYNOOK.—So be it, as Armagh says. Redbeard, show thyself a true follower of Armagh, and take this fellow to the dame on the hearth and bid her heal his wounds. Now men, disperse to thy hiding places. To-morrow night we will gather at our place of meeting, thence we will away to the depths of the dark forest beyond Cragic Head. There we will be safe from the King's men. Crassie, with six of thy sturdy fellows, see the maiden and her attendants to her place of hiding. As for myself I will meet ye at the place of meeting. Go hence, and may peace and safety attend ye all. [*They depart, leaving* BALLYNOOK *and* ARMAGH *alone.* NORAH *weeping.*]

BALLYNOOK [*to* ARMAGH].—I will go with thee until thou embark. I must e'en talk with thee.

ARMAGH.—I thank thee Ballynook. Let us depart. [*They go.*]

SCENE 3RD.—[*In front of the King's house, an assemblage of rude soldiers.* KING *comes out with his head bandaged and leaning on* McNARISH, *whom he has appointed to command the men. Old* PRIEST *follows:*

KING.—I tell thee, priest, I will go. I must drive out this villainous band of outlaws, even if I perish on the road. Bring my horse.

PRIEST.—Let us rather wait until thy strength returneth. Thou art not in condition to go abroad. Thou cans't better tarry until the morrow at the least.

KING.—Avaunt. By the powers of darkness, but I will go to-day, and now. Beware, Priest, tempt me not further. I will not brook thy objections. Villains, are ye ready. Where is Dennis? Bring him hither.

McNAGRISH.—Your Majesty. Dennis hath not been seen since the bout last night. He hath either been slain, or hath fallen into the hands of the outlaws.

KING.—Ah! the villain. More likes he has deserted me and gone to make one of the band. Now, men, hear me. He that bringeth Armagh's head to me, him will I give a hundred pieces of gold ; and to him who bringeth the head of Ballynook will I do likewise. Ye know that the promises of McMurrough are faithfully kept. But hold. If thou bringest me Ballynook alive, I will give thee two hundred pieces.

PRIEST.—Noble King, and ye men, I am as ye see, an old man. My life hath been spent in doing good, and in leading men to do better and to do no wrong. I will go with you, lest haply I may be of service. O, King, it is not right to fight and shed blood. True, if these men are outlaws, and are robbing and murdering thy subjects wantonly, then should they be banished from the earth, like vile reptiles. But can they not be reclaimed, can they not be made useful men? I pray thee, King, permit me to go among them, and lead them into the paths of virtue and usefulness.

KING.—Ah! blood and murder, but I will not endure such idle babble. Men, get ready to move straightway. Priest, keep thy babble for times of peace, and for ladies' society.

[*They all leave,* PRIEST *going with them.* HUGH *appears at side.*]

HUGH.—Ah, but it is myself that is glad to be here, instead of going yonder. I have little mind and no taste for such fighting. Right glad am I that the King forgot to take me with him. I can't understand how he made so great an oversight, but I will be content. [*A cudgel is thrown at him from side*]. Whist! Ah, but I'm murdered entirely. Stop there! Murder! Whoop! [*Enter two robbers at side*].

FIRST ROBBER.—Cease thy yelping, or by the long spoon of McGooly we will have the life of ye. Show us now where we can find some plunder, will ye? or will we be compelled to break your head by way of beginning? [*Strikes at him.*]

HUGH.—Ah! ye villain. Stop now! If ye fight with civilized weapons like that I will e'en take part myself and drive the two of ye into the bog.

[*He seizes the cudgel thrown at him, and lays about him with such effect that both robbers are knocked down, and they finally flee.* HUGH *dances an Irish jig, flourishing his cudgel.*]

SCENE 4TH.—[*In the forest,* McNAGRISH, FITZWILLIAM, *and others of the King's officers and men*].

FITZWILLIAM.—What think ye good Captain? Does Armagh fight with the greenwood men to-day? If so be it, then bad luck to us; for sorry the man will get back to the castle at all. Sure, the fates fight with him, and no man can stand before him. No better soldiers stand in the forest to-day than himself and Ballynook.

McNagrish.—No ; Armagh will not lift a finger against us. He is too shrewd a man for that. Besides, what would be the good of fighting for a handful of outlaws. Sooner or later they will be driven out or killed. No, believe me, he will not be against us to-day ; neither will Ballynook, nor Ballynook's men for that matter. Never the shoon or bounet of them will we see this day. They are secreted in the deep forest and though they be around us we will not see them. And then, do ye mind that our men have little relish to fight these merry outlaws. Half of our fellows have friends in here, and they are little minded to crack their heads. Sorry the taste of fight will we have to-day.

Fitzwilliam.—What of this old Priest who followeth us ? Sure, I think that it is bad luck anyhow to have his company. I have often heard that it was ill-favour to meet a Priest or a pig when ye went on an errand of importance. Then how much worse to have the Priest or the pig with ye.

McNagrish.—Whist, man, be quiet. There comes the Priest with the King. [*Enter* Priest, King, *and two men assisting the King.*]

McMurrough.—Captain, hath aught of the robbers been found ; or have ye any tidings of the murdering vagabonds ; the demons fly away with the pack of them.

McNagrish.—I have sent men in all directions, but not a trace of them can be found, save where they have buried the one slain by Dennis, and here is the remains of their encampment. See, it hath not been long since they were here.

McMurrough.—Oh, a murrain take them, but we will have them, if we beat the bush from here to the giant's castle.

Priest.—Good King, take my counsel, I am older than thou. Return to thy place until thy health improveth. Then, these men will be off their watch and then we can come upon them unawares. Thou art in ill case to beat the forest. Be wise and return.

McMurrogh.—Priest. I will not brook thy interference further. I command thee to molest me no more, or I will not answer for thy safety. Ha, who cometh here. [*Enter men bearing* Dennis *on a litter* ]

McMurrough.—Villain. What dost thou here. Men, where found you this fellow,

MAN.—You Majesty, we found him in a dame's cottage but just beyond the burn yonder. We thought to bring him here, seeing he might be able to tell ye where to find the outlaws.

McMURROUGH.—Speak, what dost thou here.

DENNIS [*feebly.*]—Your Majesty, I was in your service, as you remember, the night we sought the outlaws. I was already sore wounded, and fell into their hands.

McMURROUGH.—Traitor, thou liest. Had'st thou fallen into their hands, they would have slain thee, without loss of time. How camest thou to escape. Tell me that.

DENNIS.—I would not have escaped death had not Armagh besought in my behalf. He bid them bear me to the dame's cottage, then they did so.

McMURROUGH [*in a rage*].—So Armagh hath influence with the chief of the outlaws, he biddeth, and they obey. Dennis, thou art a traitor, and thy carcass shall hang from yonder tree ; up men, with him. But stay, let him remain here on his litter in the forest.

PRIEST.—Your Majesty, I see no harm this man has done. Thou said'st, to me only last night, that he that was wounded was a faithful subject of thine. It is not right to leave a dying man, alone in the forest. I will stay with him.

McMURROUGH.—Thou hast said too much to me already. If thou appeareth in my sight again, I will hang thee up in spite of thy gray hairs. Stay with him, and death to him who giveth either of them succour. Then away to the uttermost part of the forest. Depart. [*They go leaving* PRIEST *and* DENNIS *alone.*

PRIEST.—Art thou sorely wounded? I have a balsam here that doth purge and purify a wound. Let me assist thee. Art thou indeed one of the outlaws ?

DENNIS.—Venerable father, in good truth, I have so been. What is this country but a people of outlaws ? Yonder King is a robber and murderer of the vilest kind. As thou seest, he is a blood-thirsty savage, and mindeth no more to murder his loyal subjects than the outlaws. I tell thee, good father, that his great hatred against Ballynook hath been jealousy of him. Ballynook hath a daughter more fair than any in all Ireland. This monster would have wed her, but she would not. He commanded Ballynook to compel the marriage, but he refused entirely. That brought on the vengeance of McMurrough, and Ballynook must needs take to the greenwood to escape him. That is what has brought on all this trouble with the outlaws. Much more would I tell thee, but my strength faileth. O Priest, I would that I could lead an honest life.

PRIEST.—Son, thou canst be a much better man henceforth. I come to tell thy people of a better and a nobler life than that they are leading. First, however, let us heal thy bodily ills, then will I tell thee how to live aright. I fear not for thee. We will get assistance and succour in good time. Let us depend on a higher power, when all seems lost to us here. That will never fail us.

DENNIS.—Hark! Ah, they return. Father, every man who cometh is an enemy to me.—[*Enter* REDBEARD *and Crassie.*]

REDBEARD.—What meaneth this? Ha, but here is that fellow again. Venerable man, what doeth thou here with this wounded man, whom we left in a place of security? Knowest thou that the forest is filled with armed men.

PRIEST—Sir, when we get this man to a place of safety, then can I tell thee how I came hither. I know of the King's soldiers being here, as I came with them, but not of them. Come, let us bear him away.

REDBEARD—Father, thy words constrain me to do what I would not. We will bear him away for thy sake. [*They go, carrying* DENNIS *on a litter.*]

SCENE 5TH.—[*On the sea-shore, near the place of embarkation.* ARMAGH *and* BALLYNOOK *conversing.* FAHERTY, *the waterman, in a boat.*]

BALLYNOOK—Good Armagh, my spirit is disturbed to see thee depart. I would that thou wert to stay. But rest thou assured that the hearts of the people are with thee, and I am sure that no one can bind the people together as thou canst.

ARMAGH—I go, believing that it is for the best. O, that peace and quietness could come to my distracted country! O Ballynook! I love Erin more than any earthly good, willingly would I depart and remain an exile, if by so doing I could bring quietude to these shores. Ballynook, if aught should happen that it is necessary for me to return, delay not, but send at once as I bid thee. O, my loved country, fare thee well. Ballynook, farewell. [*They embrace.* ARMAGH *and* WATERMAN *leave.*]

BALLYNOOK [*to himself.*]—Ah! It is a sad day that sees thee go, thou hope of thy country. I feel that to-day I am bereft of my earthly prop and stay. I regret my past unlawful life, and it seemeth that, had I been living honestly, then would my loved son be living, and Armagh would not have been an exile. But henceforth will I live for Ireland, and for her best interests. [*Enter old* PRIEST.]

PRIEST—Son, I heard thy remarks. Knowest thou not that the paths of right and virtue are ever open and straight. There is no difficulty when thou seest aright to do that which is right. If I behold thee aright thou art the chief of what thy fellows call the outlaws.

BALLYNOOK—In truth, good sir, thou speakest aright. I am Ballynook.

PRIEST—Ballynook, thy course has been wrong. Thou hast set aside lawful authority, and hast preyed on the honest people of this land. But I know thee, and know how thou camest into this kind of life. I blame thee but little. Still, thou shouldst have taken other means to make thy livelihood. But to upbraid thee will not restore the past. Let us try to atone for the past in living better in the future. [*Enter* RED-BEARD *and* CRASSIE.]

REDBEARD [*greatly agitated*].—Good Ballynook, and ye, venerable father, away, hide ye yonder in the copse. Flee for your lives. The King cometh with his men. Leave me here to hold them. [*They retire, leaving* REDBEARD. *Enter* KING, *with* FITZWILLIAM, MCNAGRISH, *and others.*]

MCMURROUGH—Ha! Death and destruction! but who is this. O, thou double-dyed scoundrel. I know thee, though it is many days since I saw thee. On him men. Tear him limb from limb. It is Redbeard, the craftiest villain of the lot. Down with him. [REDBEARD *draws.*]

MCNAGRISH—Your majesty, it is better that we take him, and, peradventure, we may find from him where the chief of the men may be found. Let us put him under sure guard, and question him further. I will be surety for his safe delivery into thy hands.

McMurrough—The demon's whelp, but it sore distresseth me to permit him to live after he is in my power. So be it then. We will give him respite, until he lead us to the meeting place of the rest of his fellows ; bind him, and make him sure. Men, away. Haply others are in the neighbourhood, for like the wolf they hunt in packs. McNagrish, do thou talk with this fellow. Let us away. [*They go, leaving* Redbeard *with* McNagrish.]

McNagrish—Redbeard, truly am I sorry that thou art in the power of the king. Well I remember thee and thy valour. But since we have fought together I pity thee, but I tell thee truly that I have done all for thee possible. I have given thee short duration, but I know thee too well to ask thee to betray thy companions. I would e'en despise thee more heartily than I pity thee, if I thought thee capable of doing such a thing. I must likewise be loyal to my master, even the King. So I can show thee no further indulgence, only to make thy condition as easy as I can.

Redbeard.—McNagrish, thou art the same generous man thou always wast. I do not ask thee to jeopardize thyself with the King for my sake. Only, McNagrish bear to my aged sire the words which I give thee. Tell him his son would fain have died for him and for old Ireland, but as I was taken as an outlaw, I must e'en die as an outlaw. But tell him that I die without fear, and that at the last I defied the tyrant McMurrough to his teeth. I thank thee for these few hours of life that thou hast granted me, McNagrish. I know not how this man may appoint me to die, but after he has done his worst, I ask thee as the last friend I have near me, to take the charm which you will find on my breast, suspended by a gold cord, and take it to Kathleen who lives in the dell, hard by Craggie Head, And tell her that my last thoughts on earth were of her, and of old Ireland.

McNagrish.—Stop, thou wilt make a woman of me, Redbeard. I, too, love old Ireland, and ask no higher fate than that my blood be spilt for her. Yes, I will e'en do as thou sayest. I will bear thy messages for thee. Yea, good comrade, though it be at the cost of my life will I bear thy messages. Now, let us away. [*They go out.*]

## PART THIRD.

SCENE 1ST.—[*In the audience chamber of the King,* ETHELRED *of Britain. Present*—ANDELWALD, EDGAR (*the King's brother*), ESTELLA (*a beautiful maiden, the King's sister.*)      KING *speaks,* (*King a youth.*)]

ETHELRED.—How sayest thou, Andelwald. Cometh again to our shores the noble Armagh. It is well that he cometh. He is a good man and a true, and cometh with no evil intent: Ah, that all men came as doth he. My mind is sore troubled with the evil intentions of men about me. I knew not how vile and wicked was the heart of man until I were a king. And more I learn every day of this evil intent in man. Good Andelwald, I would I were a shepherd boy, to rove through the blooming vales and meet no worse companions than my sheep. Then would I be happy, so that Edgar and Estella were by my side. When Armagh cometh, bring him hither, that I may ask him how speedeth the people of our neighbouring land.

ANDELWALD.—I think he is hard by. But small welcome would he get did he wait for Andelwald to bid him come in peace. A man of his import cometh not through all the dangers of the sea on idle errand. Believe me, your majesty, he cometh for no good. Being older and more experienced in the wickedness that thou speakest of, I would set spies upon him, to guard the object of his visit. Great King, I know his master, e'en that crafty fox, Dermot McMurrough. I know that he scrupleth not to slay whosoever he is minded. It is but morning recreation for him to hang up a squad of his courtiers to make amusement for the survivors. Thus keeping in mind the brutal nature of the King, what should we expect of his chief captain and adviser.

ESTELLA.—Good Andelwald, I remember well this man thou speakest of. I saw him when he abode in the court of our uncle, the former king. He was then a man of most likely and noble presence ; his conversation was of a dignified and impressible order ; likewise were his words full of wisdom and gentleness. He may come on missions of mercy, and surely he deserveth not our censure until we know some what of wrong against him.

EDGAR [*a hot, impulsive boy*].—So talk all women. Hath a man a pleasant face and lordly carriage, then will the female folk see nought but good in him. Were I King as thou art, brother, I would send this Irish lord howling back to his native bogs, or I would pitch him heels and neck into the sea.

ETHELRED.—Boy, be still. Learn to curb thy wayward tongue ; or who can answer for the safety of thy empty head. Sister, thy speech is far beyond thy years and sex for wisdom. Andelwald, bring the noble prince hither at thy convenience, I must speak with him. Brother, go thou bring the aged Cambrian harper that he may sing to me of the glories of the olden time. [*Andelwald and Edgar go out.*]

ETHELRED.—Gentle sister, I would that I had such a prince beside me as this noble Armagh. I feel no fear to meet him, although I know him not. He is a man of peace and wisdom. That agreeth with my nature far better than war and blood. Some that come and fawn upon me, fill me with a nameless dread and terror. So do these Druid Priests, these men of blood and death. O sister! tell me the story of that new unknown belief, that is full of peace and gentleness.

ESTELLA.—Thou art now a King, and must be a King in thy manner, and according to the custom of these times. It is not meet that these courtiers and sturdy men-at-arms should hear thee speak thus. 'Tis well that none heareth thee but me, or else they would revile thee. However, thou canst be a better king if thou bearest in thy heart the teachings of this new religion. Hark! some one cometh. [*Enter* HARPER, *an old man, with boy bearing his harp, and* EDGAR.]

EDGAR.—Here, noble brother, is the Harper, who will discourse pleasant music to thy liking. As for me, with thy permission, I will depart hence, to hunt the hare with thy Forester.

ETHELRED.—Go, and may peace and safety attend thee. And thou, venerable father, I trust thou art in good and wholesome case to-day ?

HARPER [*making obeisance*].—Mighty King, thy servant hath not aught in that behalf to complain. I have sufficient food, proper shelter, and no grievous pain distresseth me.

ETHELRED.—Wilt thou sing unto me of the glories of the
elder days ?   But first let me sustain thee with this wholesome
draught.   [KING *pours out a flagon of liquid and hands him.
He drinks.*]

HARPER.—Ah, but there is new life in that precious draught.
It warms the old blood in my veins, and maketh my heart to
be young again.   May health and long life attend thee, and
the gentle maiden at thy side.   Now will I sing thee a song
that no man within these borders hath heard since thy grandfather sat upon thy throne.   [*He sings, accompanying himself on
the harp.   Song in the ancient Cambrian tongue.   Interval.   Noise
outside.   Enter* ANDELWALD, *with* ARMAGH.   *Harper ceases.*]

ETHELRED.—Andelwald, thou art welcome.   Bringest thou
the noble Prince of Ireland ?

ANDELWALD.—Yea, my lord, this is he.   [ARMAGH *bows.*]

ETHELRED.—Noble Armagh, right glad am I to meet thee,
and bid thee welcome to my kingdom.   Thou art more than
welcome, noble Prince.

ARMAGH.—Mighty King, there is no more welcome task to
me than to greet thee.   The fame of thy youthful wisdom and
valour, and of thy regard for thy subjects hath penetrated even
to the remotest nations.

ETHELRED.—Enough, good Armagh.   Thou must be my
guest whilst thou tarriest here.   Dost thou regard the chase ?
Then my gentle brother will guide thee through the forest in
quest of the fleeing deer, or with nimble hawk bring down the
lofty heron for thy pleasure.   Now will we hear the residue of
the worthy father's song, which was broken by thy entrance.
Father, complete thy song.   [HARPER *sings and plays.   Scene
closes.*]

SCENE 2ND.—[*In the forest of Ireland, near the Outlaws' place
of meeting.   Enter* FITZWILLIAM *and others of the* KING'S *men,
with* BALLYNOOK, *captive.*]

FITZWILLIAM.—Men, gently with this one.   I think me that
from his look he is no common man among the merry greenwood men.   But it is bad luck to be hunting the likes of him.
He is a fine-looking man.   Ah, but he is a brave one, too.
Did'st thou see that he scorned to flee from us ?   Sure, but I
am minded to let him depart in peace, for he may be the lord
of some of these lands beyond.   Speak, friend.   Art thou an
honest man, and not one of the outlaws whom we seek ?

BALLYNOOK.—Fitzwilliam, I scorn to lie to thee, as I did to flee from thee. Thou hast an honest heart, but I ask not aught of favour of thee. Do thy King's command, even to slay me.

FITZWILLIAM [*to his fellows*].—Ah, but it is the fine-spoken gentleman that he is, and no robber. Sir [*to* BALLYNOOK], it is after asking your pardon that we are, and a good speed on your journey, and prosperous luck to the business ye was driving.

BALLYNOOK.—Since you are so good as to bid me, I will go. But mind, it is thy own wish that I depart. [*Noise, trumpets and voices. Enter* MCMURROUGH, *with* MCNAGRISH, *and others.*]

MCMURROUGH.—Bad luck to the villainous robbers! My head is bursting with the pain of hunting the forest. Here is Fitzwilliam and my trusty men. Ah! blood and murder! Do I see him? Give me a spear! [*He snatches a spear from a soldier and rushes at* BALLYNOOK. FITZWILLIAM *throws himself before* BALLYNOOK.]

FITZWILLIAM.—Your Majesty, stay! This is a worthy gentleman we detained through ignorance. Let me speak. [KING *more enraged, strikes with vengeance at* BALLYNOOK, *kills* FITZWILLIAM, *and mortally wounds* BALLYNOOK. *Then, through excess of rage and his former hunt, swoons away. Men scatter, some bearing off the* KING. *They leave* FITZWILLIAM'S *body and* BALLYNOOK *on the ground.*]

SCENE 3.—[*In the Dame's Cottage.* BALLYNOOK *upon the bed, dying.* NORAH *weeping over him, other maidens present weeping.* REDBEARD, CRASSIE *and other outlaws. Dame, (old woman) ministering unto the dying man. He calls* REDBEARD.]

BALLYNOOK.—My faithful well-tried friend; I would, were it possible, that the venerable Priest speak to me. If he come I would spend the last fleeting moments of my life with him. But while I have the strength I would charge thee to take this ring, bear it to Faherty the waterman, take with it also my bow string that is red with my blood, and bid him take them straightway to Armagh. Didst thou understand good Redbeard?

REDBEARD.—Yea, my friend, I do. [*He weeps.*]

BALLYNOOK.—And, Redbeard, whilst thou hast life in thy body, I charge thee never to forsake my only remaining child, my daughter Norah, until she hath a proper place of safety. Now let her come hither. My daughter, thy father hath fought his last battle, and soon will be no more. I charge thee to remember the good he hath done and not the bad. I would that I could live for thy sake, but thou knowest I am near death. [*Enter attendants with the carcass of a calf and with materials to kindle the Banshee light, to frighten away the bad spirits and to light the departing soul to the happy abode of the good. Attendants set up a wailing. Enter* OUTLAW *with* OLD PRIEST.]

BALLYNOOK.—Good father, I am glad to see thee come. Sure, I have come to a part of the journey where I am in the dark and require a guide and assistance. The darkness is coming upon me, and I need a light. Canst thou give it?

PRIEST.—I will do what remaineth for human power to do. Leave me with this dying man and his child. [*They all go out but* NORAH *and* PRIEST. *Scene closes. Curtain drops. Interval, and Curtain raises on same scene, with Norah and attendant maidens weeping over the body of* BALLYNOOK. *Banshee fire burning. Outlaws waking the body*]

SCENE 4TH.—[*In* ETHELRED'S *Court again.* ETHELRED ANDELWALD, *and* ESTELLA *present*].

ETHELRED.—How thinkest thou, good Andelwald, of the Irish Prince now?

ANDELWALD.—Your Majesty, I must say he bears himself right nobly for his former education. He speaketh discreetly, and seemeth to be a good man.

ESTELLA.—Thou art right, and no one can see him but will think as thou thinkest. [*Enter* EDGAR *noisily.*]

ETHELRED.—Whence comest thou now, youngster, with such bluster and lack of ceremony? Canst thou not mend thy pace when thou enterest our presence?

EDGAR.—Pardon me, royal brother, but I think of thee most as my loving brother, and not as my lawful King.

ETHELRED.—Thou art welcome to come as thou pleasest. I did but jest with thee. But whence art thou?

EDGAR.—I come but just from the fields where I hunted with thy noble guest, the Irish Prince. He is a fine gentleman, and I would that he hunted with me every day. He hath entertained me most royally, besides he hath a merry heart for the sports of the field. Twice this day the fleeing deer would have sped from me, but his strong bow and unerring arrow stopped it. Canst thou not bid him stay, and dwell in our country, which is far better than the land he hath left. I will e'en now go fetch him in. [EDGAR *leaves* ]

ETHELRED.—So it seemeth that this man hath made a conquest, his royal master, the doughty McMurrough, could not have made. He hath won the good will of my impulsive brother, as well as thine, Andelwald. But here he cometh with Edgar. [*Enter* ARMAGH, *making obeisance to the* KING *and* ESTELLA.]

ETHELRED.—Armagh, welcome, how fared the sport to-day? To judge of what Edgar saith, thou art slaying all my deer.

ARMAGH.—Your Majesty, well have I enjoyed the pleasures of this day, and the pleasant companionship of thy brother. He hath a merry heart, and is a most honourable sportsman. He always giveth the deer a chance to escape with his life.

ETHELRED.—Aye, truly ; and most frequently do they improve his generous chance, and speed them away.

EDGAR.—Brother, thou knowest that I often bring thee a royal haunch of most excellent venison, besides other small game.

ETHELRED.—Truly thou dost, especially when such hunters as our friend Armagh go with thee. But we will talk of weightier matters. Good Armagh, how speedeth the people of thy land. Hath the King secured the love and respect of his subjects ?

ARMAGH [*sadly*].—Ah, noble King. Him thou see'st before thee, hath no land, no country, and no King. I am an outcast from the land of my fathers. I am an exile, having incurred the displeasure of the King.

ETHELRED.—Armagh, I am much astonished as well as grieved to hear thee speak thus. Again, am I glad, for here canst thou remain and be a member of our household. Yea, good Armagh, abide with us. Thou art more than welcome.

EDGAR.—Hurrah ! stay with us ; we will go hunting every day.

ETHELRED.—Peace. Keep thy noise and hallooing for

thy chase in the forest. But hark ! Andelwald wilt thou go and find the cause of such unseemly disturbance outside. [*He goes and presently returns with English soldiers, leading a rough Irishman.*]

IRISHMAN.—I tell thee that I will fight the lot of ye, only give me the blackthorn splinter that I had in old Ireland. May the saints preserve my eyes till I see her again. And it's a burning shame to ye not to know how to treat a gentleman who comes only to be speaking to so fine a gentleman as the great Armagh, bad luck to ye all for beggarly thieves to be leading a man around like a bullock by the horns at a fair, to be gazed at and stroked by every body. Away now and hands off me for a fair showing and I will fight the lot of ye.

ETHELRED.—Percy, whence came ye with this man, and what have ye done to him ? I perceive he is a citizen of our neighbouring land.

PERCY [*a soldier*].—Your Majesty, we found him wandering in the forest and calling for Armagh. We deemed him mad, and brought him hither for thee to judge what shall be done with him. [*Soldiers go out.*]

ARMAGH [*coming forward*].—Let me see this man. This voice is familiar to me. Ah ! [*astonished*] It is, Hugh. Good fellow, what doest thou here ?

HUGH [*breaking away and embracing* ARMAGH].—Ah your honour, but its surely dreaming, that I am. Somebody strike me and see if I waken. May the saints keep me safe until I see another so welcome a sight as you honour's face. Sure, it is speechless I am with joy at meeting ye in this vagabond and heathenish land. Bad luck to the villains for trotting me about for the entertainment of the gaping crowd of heathens.

ARMAGH.—Easy, Hugh, see'st thou that thou art now in the presence of the King, and the ladies of the court. I shall be ashamed that thou art a countryman of mine.

HUGH.—Bad luck to me for a vagabond if I have offended his majesty or the ladies. Sure, I will be after axing pardon if you will introduce me to the King, and the ladies.

ARMAGH.—Your majesty, this man hath been in the service of Dermot McMorrough, and I knew him to be an honest and faithful fellow. I know not how he came hither. We will ask him.

HUGH. — Ah and is it the fine gentleman you were after speaking to, the King. Your majesty, long life to your honour, and may the snakes crawl off with the vagabond that spakes ill of ye, at all, or the fine young lady who I consate is your majesty's sister, as ye both have the same sparkling eyes. Sure I am killed entirely for fear I have spoken too rudely. I hope your honour will give me time to speak with the noble Armagh before ye hang me. Ah [*shuddering*], but it was near I came to it over yonder.

ETHELRED. — Friend, fear no harm. Only collect thy scattered wits and tell us how camest thou hither?

HUGH. — Ah, but it is long life to your majesty for a pleasant spoken gentleman, and may my right arm drop off, but I would fight a host of such blaggards. I beg your honour's pardon, such gentlemen as brought me in for ye. Sure, I am faint for drink, as may the saints keep the drop I have tasted since yesterday, barring a half-dozen or so times.

ETHELRED. — Give him to drink, attend to his wants, then tell us, Hugh, thy journey to Britain, [*They give him a flagon, and he drinks long, and with considerable noise.*]

HUGH. — Ah, but it is no wonder that your majesty is so handsome and rosy, when ye drink such as that. Sure, but it brings the life back to me and I feel braver than I have for this twelve month. Sorry the bit of water would pass my lips did I get the likes every day. I'll take another sup. [*He drinks again.*]

ETHELRED. — Now, Hugh, I see thou art much refreshed, and altogether a new man. Thou hast nothing to fear, now without any waste of words tell us how camest thou in the forest, when we thought thee in the service of the good King Dermot.

HUGH. — May the demons possess all such good kings as he, hoping your majesty and the ladies will not tell him I said so, for he is in a bad humour anyhow. But the noble Armagh [*may the saints preserve him*] knows how that the King hath been fighting the robbers and outlaws. Well, then he got worsted and was brought home all bloody and insensible and with his head broke as elegantly as I could have done it myself with a stick.

ARMAGH.—Cut thy story short, and tell plainly how thou camest to leave thy place.

HUGH.—Well, then, after that, he would collect the men together and go out, in spite of myself and the old priest and everybody else. Sure it was the towering rage he was in, and he with his head tied up, but off they all posted, and left me alone in the home, when two vagabond thieves came in, and I took a bit of a switch and broke the heads of the two of them.

ARMAGH.—Hugh, tell at once how thou camest hither?

HUGH.—As I told thee they went off, old priest and all, and on the second day following, save one, sure they returned the same way, only the King this time did not come to himself until the fourth day after, only roaring and groaning with the fever and the pain. O, but it was troublesome times when he began to come to himself. Sure, but he would call for his sword, or a spear, and nobody durst disobey him, then he would throw the spear at the first man he could see. Sure but it is the dragon's own boy he is now. Well, then one day the priest came to leech him, and the priest told him that he had such a hurt in his back, that with the riding and the exposure in the night, and the hunt and all that, that he never could walk again, then but for his escaping would the King have killed him entirely. As it was, it was dangerous for anyone to go in. At last he sent for me, and I went to the door all trembling, for I didn't know but he would take the life of me. And he says, said he, my dear good Hugh wilt thou help me out of the bed? When I tried to lift him I was so frightened of him that I slipped and let him drop in the bed. Ah, but it was then that he roared, and I made off with all speed, but I heard him order me to be hanged without any ceremony; and sure but I kept running till I came to the sea coast, and I hired with the boatman there who was about to leave, and after coming near being drowned with the wind and the water, I was put ashore in this beggarly country asking your majesty's pardon, and the ladies. And the soldiers picked me up and mistreated me, and pulled me about, until they brought me here, and here I am. And to be sure, your majesty will not be after sending me back to be hanged at all.

ETHELRED.—No, good Hugh, you shall not be sent back.

You shall remain here as long as ye like. Here men, take him and supply his wants. [*They take him out.*]

SCENE 5TH.—[*In* DERMOT MCMURROUGH'S *house, in his bed chamber.* MCMURROUGH *in bed, propped up with pillows.*]

MCMURROUGH (*calls*).—Ho, villains, cravens ! where are ye gone. Would ye be leaving a man to die alone in his bed. I will murder the last one of ye when I am out of this. [*Enter a Druid Priest making obeisance.*].

PRIEST.—How fares it with your majesty to-day ?

MCMURROUGH.—Ha, well may you ask, when you all shun me as if I were a beast that would tear ye.

PRIEST.—I come every day, your majesty, to see thee. Thou art too violent in thy mind, calm thyself and thou wilt be better.

MCMURROUGH [*reaching for weapons.*].—Villain ! I will spike thee to the wall for thy insolence.

PRIEST.—Hold ! Man thou art distempered. Would'st thou lift a hand against the Priest of the sacred grove ? Why would'st thou murder me, when I come to do thee good ? Nay, give me thy weapons. Now hear me, McMurrough. Would'st thou ever stand on thy feet and be a man again ? Hast thou a desire to mount thy horse and do battle against thy enemies ? then must thou curb thyself and be less a savage monster. Thy people leave thee because thou art so fierce and cruel to them. Who would enter here when thou hast thy weapons, and casts them at every one who enters ?

MCMURROUGH.—Avaunt, false, lying knave. Leave my sight, and may the demons take me but I will give orders that the hated brood of Priests shall be destroyed, and thy groves and temples burnt to the ground. Ho, there, attendant. [*Attendant comes.*]

MCMURROUGH.—Stand not there but send me McNagrish. [PRIEST *and attendant go out.*] Ha, the dragons take the vile disease that keeps me here, when I have so much to do. Oh, the vile brood of vipers ! I will crush them, if I hang and slay every Priest and villainous outlaw on this island. [*Enter* MCNAGRISH.]

MCMURROUGH.—McNagrish, thou art my only remaining stay, my only hold on the government of this country. Knowest thou aught of the whereabouts of Armagh ?

McNagrish.—I know not, save I have heard that he has crossed to Britain.

McMurrough.—Ah! He has gone to the court of the mighty Ethelred. I wonder hath he entered the service of that downy youth. Ah, may the saints despise the days when shepherd lads are Kings. But then, good Captain, it is better than a warlike man were King.

McNagrish.—I know little, save that I heard from some one that Armagh was after cultivating the soil, and leading a herdsman's life in that country.

McMurrough.—Well, so be it. It is better than he was fighting us. Dost thou know, McNagrish, that it was indeed Armagh that struck me the blow that was the cause of all this distemper. But it surely was he for no other man in the seven kingdoms can strike so heavily. McNagrish, I loved that man as he were my only brother. Why think you did he turn against me, and in behalf of the murdering outlaw?

McNagrish.—I know not. But let us talk of other matters, or better still not talk at all. Hast thou any commands? Would'st thou that I call anyone?

McMurrough.—Yea, since thou hast spoken, call me the old Priest that was with me at the time of the last fight with the outlaws. I would speak with him. Knowest thou of him?

McNagrish.—Yea, I have heard somewhat of him. He healeth many diseases among the people, and many follow after him and he speaketh often to them. His words are wisdom, and he teacheth a new doctrine, even that we should fight no more but forgive the injuries our enemies do us. [*Voice outside.*]

Voice.—Woe unto the men of blood. Their days shall be consumed in pain, and their nights shall go down in darkness.

McMurrough.—Bad luck to me, but what is that! Good Captain, go outside and see who it is that insulteth me thus in mine own house. [McNagrish *goes out.*]

## PART FOURTH.

SCENE 1ST.—[*In the forest in England,* ARMAGH *and* EDGAR, *the King's brother, in hunting costume.* HUGH *following behind.*]

HUGH [*talking to himself*].—Bad cess to the villainous country that this is. Sure a man don't get such to eat as the dogs in old Ireland hide in the earth. The bones of me are rattling with starvation. Ah! but who comes yonder. By the holy poker, it is Faherty. [HUGH *runs to embrace him. Enter* FAHERTY.]

FAHERTY.—May the saints defend me but it is Hugh. Be easy now, will you, till I speak to his Honour, the noble Armagh. Long life to your honour. [*He bows before* ARMAGH.]

ARMAGH.—Ha! speak man. Thou bearest tidings. Good Faherty, tell me quickly thy summons.

FAHERTY.—Here, I have a packet for thee which I have carried in my bosom from across the sea. [*He gives packet to* ARMAGH.]

ARMAGH [*opens packet*].—Ah, my bleeding country, but it is my own ring, and by this token she calls me home. What is this? It is Ballynook's bowstring, and red with blood. I understand the import of this. Edgar bear my going to your royal brother and to your sister. I must away with this man. To-day my country calls me and I must not idle here. Noble youth, farewell. [EDGAR *weeps and falls upon his neck.*]

EDGAR.—Noble sir, I will not leave thee. Let me bear thee company across the sea. I cannot part from thee.

ARMAGH.—Son, it cannot be. Thou knowest not the state of the people there. Thou art too young to go now, and the times are too much troubled for thee to go. Nay, abide here until peace returns to our borders, then shalt thou come and live with me. [EDGAR *still clings to him.*]

EDGAR.—O, noble Armagh, I shall not see thee again, if thou leavest me, I will not leave thee unless thou command me.

ARMAGH.—Then, Edgar, I command thee to stay. It teareth me to leave thee, but I must go. Here I leave with thee my trusty friend Hugh, who will come with thee when it is proper for thee. Good Hugh, remain with the lad and share his sports.

HUGH.—I will, your honour, as ye ask me to, but will ye be telling the King that I always spake well of him, and that there's no occasion for him to be hanging me for dropping him in the bed.

ARMAGH.—Hugh, keep thou the young man safe, and remember to speak always discreetly and speak but little. And when peace shall prevail in our country. I would have thee return. Farewell! good friend! Edgar, thou hast the heart of a hero. Thou knowest not the unsettled state of my land. Be of good cheer [*embraces him*]. Good honest Hugh, farewell [*shakes* HUGH's *hand*]. [*Exit* ARMAGH *and* FAHERTY. EDGAR *throws hemself on the ground.*]

EDGAR.—O Hugh, thou knowest not how I love the noble Armagh. He is the light of my life, and all is darkness when he is gone. Oh, what shall I do, I love my brother, but he is not of my mind. His mind runneth to the society of ladies and of the soft and tender things of peace and books. My gentle sister even is more warlike than he. But Armagh, is of my mind. He is a soldier. He hath fought on the Black Moor, and his words stir me at times like the note of battle. But we will join him, Hugh. We will prepare and go forth with him to fight.

HUGH.—That we will, my lad. Sure, but will we take our sticks and sorry a head will we leave not cracked at all, and when he marches in to be the King, we will follow with the rest, with our hats on our sticks, and singing like father Jack Welch at the fair [*they go out*].

SCENE 2ND.—[*In Ireland. Near the King's house in the forest. Enter* MCNAGRISH, *and others of the King's soldiers.*]

MCNAGRISH.—Brian, hast thou heard the tidings of the coming of Teague. He hath heard of the illness of our master and he cometh with great force, to overthrow us, and murder McMurrough in his bed. Sure, but I think the times will be hard for us and no one to lead the men to battle. It will not be proper to tell the King, or he will be after trying to mount his horse and lead us to battle. There is one man whom I wish to see in Old Ireland.

BRIAN.—Sure, but I read thy thoughts. Thou speakest of Armagh.

McNAGRISH.—Brian. Thou art right. Though Dermot McMurrough be thy mother's son, yet I tell thee that he was too rash with Armagh. He hath a noble spirit, and will not be trodden upon.

BRIAN.—My brother hath a violent spirit, and would as quickly hurl a dart through me as through the meanest slave in the land. We must remember that [*enter* SOLDIER *breathless*].

SOLDIER.—Hark ye good captain, and ye, noble Brian. Sure, there cometh beyond the long bog, the bloody Teague of Leath, and he burneth and slayeth before him. He hath above a thousand men, and the people are perishing before him. Ah bad luck to us, but we will all be murdered entirely.

McNAGRISH.—Good Brian, what shall we do, Sure it will never do to tell the King of the troubles. Here, friend. Set a guard about the King's house, and see that none passeth, nor that no tidings be brought the King [*enter old* PRIEST *unperceived*], Brian we must endeavour to rally the men together [PRIEST *comes forward*].

PRIEST.—Good friend, peace be to thee. Thou art troubled, and well thou mayest be, for but few men stand before Teague of Leath. There is one man who can bind the people together as one man, and in whose good right arm stays the strength of a hundred Teagues. If thou wilt, I will bring him hither, for he is hard by.

BRIAN.—Father, as the brother of the King, and having his authority during his sickness, I bid thee bring this man. [PRIEST *goes out, and returns soon with* ARMAGH. BRIAN *and* McNAGRISH *salute him warmly.*]

BRIAN.—Sir, thou art, I know, a true and lawful son of Erin. Thou art not willing to see her people perish. We have no time to waste in words. Here is the ancient sword of the Kings of Ireland. Take it, and lead the people against their enemies.

ARMAGH.—Brian, my arm is ever ready to strike for my country. I know no higher duty than her service. But I would much better fight with the people, and thou, the King's brother, command.

BRIAN.—I will not. Here, take the sword. And thou, McNagrish, go forth and make proclamation to the people to come forth and fight for their homes, and for their King, and for Armagh. [MCNAGRISH *goes.* PRIEST *goes another way.*]

BRIAN.—Armagh, thou most likely heard that the King hath a severe illness, and all these things must be kept from him. Likewise, begging pardon of your honour, he must not know that thou art here.

ARMAGH.—I should not have returned, only that there was occasion of war. But we have not time for idle talk. Let us away and prepare for the battle. [*They go out.*]

SCENE 3RD.—[*In the open field, hard by the Long Bog.* AR-MAGH *in the garb of battle, with drawn sword in his hand.* BRIAN *and* MCNAGRISH, REDBEARD, *and many others standing around. Noise of shouting and trumpets in the distance.*]

ARMAGH.—Men, hear ye yonder the noise of the coming of the invaders. Behind ye lieth the homes ye have left, with the women and children of your bosoms looking to ye for protection. This day must these homes be made desolate, or the enemies of your King and country must be driven back. Do I speak to men, or to cravens and cowards? [*All speak.*]

ALL.—Lead us, noble Armagh. [*Enter* HUGH *flourishing a cudgel.*]

HUGH.—Bad luck to me, but I must fight with the bold Armagh. [*Enter* EDGAR, *throwing himself into* ARMAGH'S *arms.*]

EDGAR.—I will fight by thy side until thou conquer thy enemies.

ARMAGH.—Rash youth, how camest thou hither? But thou must away. Go, I command thee, to the rear of the battle. [EDGAR *goes reluctantly away.* HUGH *goes with him at the command of* ARMAGH.]

ARMAGH.—Men, every one to his duty. Go forth, and may victory and success go with you. [*All go but* ARMAGH *and* BRIAN. *Great noise of battle outside.* *Men come carrying dead and wounded men to the rear.* BRIAN *goes hastily out.* DEN-NIS *appears, and bows to* ARMAGH.]

DENNIS.—Noble sir, this day would I prove to thee that I am a true son of Erin. I would that thou permit me to fight.

ARMAGH,—Go, good Dennis, thy country needs thee in the

battle. [DENNIS *draws sword and goes out.* ARMAGH *follows him. Interval. Great noise of battle. They still bear the wounded bleeding to the rear. Enter* TEAGUE OF LEATH, *an enormous man with a large sword reeking with blood.*]

TEAGUE.—Ha ! Murder and destruction ! Show me the champion of this people. Where now is the noble Armagh. I am Teague of Leath, and no one durst stand before me. Let him come. He feareth the face of the mighty Teague of Leath. Whoop ! [TEAGUE *flourishes his sword, and calls for some- one to meet him. Enter* ARMAGH, *with the sword of the* KING *in his hand.*]

ARMAGH.— Vile boaster, this day shalt the ground which thou desecrated with thy presence drink thy blood. Villain, defend thyself. [TEAGUE *strikes a terrible blow at him.* AR- MAGH *parries the blow, and they go to battle.* ARMAGH *crowds* TEAGUE *back, but slips and falls backward.*]

TEAGUE.—Now I have thee. Now thou diest. [*He aims a blow at* ARMAGH'S *breast, but* EDGAR *rushes out, throws himself on* ARMAGH, *and is slain by the sword of* TEAGUE. HUGH, *following* EDGAR, *strikes the Rebel Chief a furious stroke with his cudgel, and* ARMAGH *slays* TEAGUE *with his sword. The followers of* TEAGUE *flee when they see their leader fall. Gen- eral rout of* TEAGUE'S *men.* ARMAGH *kneeling by* EDGAR'S *body, weeps o'er him. Enter* COURIER *breathless.*]

COURIER.—Your honour, the enemy flee, and our soldiers follow cutting them in pieces. [*Enter* BRIAN.]

ARMAGH.—Brian, go thou and command the people. See that they stay not until the invaders are driven from our soil. As for myself, I am overcome with grief. Here is the body of a noble youth, who died that I might live. Leave me alone with him.

BRIAN.—It shall be done. The enemy is defeated, their chief is slain, and we will drive the remnant of them out of our borders. Thou has fought to good purpose to-day. [BRIAN *goes.*]

HUGH.—Indeed we have fought well. It is sad that the fine young man's slain. He was too rash for his own safety. Ha, that is my opinion that for good fighting a bit of a black- thorn stick is far superior to anything else.

[HUGH *brings a mantle and wraps the body of* EDGAR. *Then it is borne out, followed by* ARMAGH. *Dirge music outside.*]

SCENE 4th [In DERMOT MCMURROUGH'S *bedchamber.* KING *pale and anxious. He is feeble and much reduced. Talks to himself.*]

MCMURROUGH.—Ha, there is somewhat that is wrong. Methinks I have heard unwonted noises, and it seemeth like the sound of battle. I must know how matters progresseth outside. Ho, there, ye sleepy villain. [*Enter attendant.*]

ATTENDANT [*keeping near the door*]. Did your Majesty call ?

KING.—Did I call ? Yea, caitiff, loud enough to waken the priests in the old temple down by the sea. Is my brother Brian near at hand ?

ATTENDANT.—Yea, he did but now enter the grounds, beyond thy house.

KING.—Bid him enter. I would speak with him. [*Attendant retires and* BRIAN *enters.*]

BRIAN.—Fair and softly, noble Dermot. Thou seemest in a fever of excitement. Calm thyself. Hath the old Priest called upon thee to-day ?

DERMOT.—A murrain take the old Priest and his mummeries. I hate the lot of them. But I would not speak to thee of such things, Brian. Tell me the truth, or despite thy kinship to me, thou shalt rue it, if thou holdest back aught. There is something of great moment in the land. Thou durst not hold it back from me. Speak man !

BRIAN.—It is naught. We but had a brush with the men of Leath, and drove them back to the borders. Think not of it. The like happeneth continually, in the unsettled state of our times.

MCMURROUGH [*much excited*].—Ha ! Sir, would ye to battle without speaking of it to me. Villains all. My own brother is against me !

BRIAN.—Dermot, consider thyself, whether thou art in condition to lead men to battle. We kept it from thee for thy own good. The enemy is driven out, and their leader slain.

MCMURROUGH.—What, Teague of Leath slain. Brian lie not to me.

BRYAN.—I lie not. Teague is now dead, since thou must know all the tidings.

McMURROUGH [*greatly excited*].—Ha, the demons fly away with him. Brian, thou hast nobly fought. I thank thee. Thou didst lead the people to be sure. No one else but a McMurrough would have conquered and slain the valiant Teague. Speak, then, didst lead the people, and bear the o'd sword of the Kings of Ireland?

BRIAN.—Thou art too greatly excited for thy good. Rest in peace until the morrow. Thou hast the important news and nothing further of moment remaineth to be told to thee.

McMURROUGH.—Thou hast not answered me. Thou evadest the question. Brian, didst thou command the people?

BRIAN.—Since thou must have answer, and will not rest otherwise, I did not. Now go to thy rest, and at some time when thou art better able to hear, I will give thee a history of the battle.

McMURROUGH.—Sir, I will know who led the people and slew the great Teague. Was it McNagrish?

BRIAN.—Nay! Canst thou not consider thy own condition. Thou art wrought up to the remotest pitch. Let me go. Farewell.

McMURROUGH.—Stay. I am Dermot McMurrough. I am King of Ireland, and all power is in my hands. I command thee to speak and tell me who commanded the people. [*Enter old* PRIEST.] Ah! Brian! it was the old Priest? Tell me!

BRIAN.—It was not. Why art thou so violent? It was not the Priest.

McMURROUGH.—I command thee then to speak, or fear my displeasure.

BRIAN.—I will tell thee, then wilt thou go to rest. It was Armagh! [McMURROUGH *gasps for breath, tries to speak, throws up his hands and falls back dead.* BRIAN *and* PRIEST *raise him, but, seeing him dead, lay him down and covered him.*]

SCENE 5TH.—[ARMAGH *walking alone in the forest. Talking to himself.*]

ARMAGH.—It must not be. Down false ambition, I will join the good old Priest, and spend the remainder of my life, leading my countrymen into the paths of peace and rectitude, I will go first to Britain, and tell the gentle Ethelred and his noble sister, how the loved Edgar came to his death. O woe is me ! I loved the generous youth as my son. [*He weeps.*] No! I must not be King of this people. Brian hath the natural right, and he will be a good and a wise king, for he already hearkeneth to the wise counsels of the good Priest. [*Enter* BRIAN, MCNAGRISH, REDBEARD *now one of the King's men*], *and others.*]

BRIAN.—Noble sir, we seek you to place upon you the mantle of the King of Ireland. The people desire it, and as the natural successor to the kingdom, I freely relinquish all right in thy favour. Armagh, bid us proclaim thee King of Ireland. [*Enter old Priest.*]

ARMAGH.—It cannot be. My course is already before me. Brian, thou art the proper man to succeed thy brother. I cannot. I go with the Priest who stands beside me. It shall be our duty to lead the people from darkness they now are in, and into the light of truth and virtue. Henceforth Armagh lives not for his own glory, but that the world may be better for his having lived in it. McNagrish do thou and those with thee now place the royal robe upon Brian. [*They place the royal robe upon* BRIAN, *old* PRIEST *spreads his hands over him, all kneel to* BRIAN, *slow music outside, curtain falls.*]

END OF DERMOT MCMURROUGH.